WILLIAM MORRIS

William Morris was born in London, England in 1834. Arguably best known as a textile designer, he founded a design partnership which deeply influenced the decoration of churches and homes during the early 20th century. However, he is also considered an important Romantic writer and pioneer of the modern fantasy genre, being a direct influence on authors such as J. R. R. Tolkien. As well as fiction, Morris penned poetry and essays. Amongst his best-known works are *The Defence of Guenevere and Other Poems* (1858), *The Earthly Paradise* (1868–1870), *A Dream of John Ball* (1888), *News from Nowhere* (1890), and the fantasy romance *The Well at the World's End* (1896). Morris was also an important figure in British socialism, founding the Socialist League in 1884. He died in 1896, aged 62.

PREFACE

THE three excellent Icelandic stories that are printed first in this book were, in their present form at least, written respectively in the thirteenth, the fourteenth, and the fifteenth centuries: the earliest of them, the *Gunnlaug*, has even been assigned by tradition to Ari the Learned, the father of Icelandic history: the names of people and the genealogies given in it, as well as the names given to their habitations, are found to agree with what we learn about them from other early records; and, in short, it must be called an historical tale, in spite of anything marvellous or mythological that is to be found in it.

The *Frithiof*, on the other hand, is an example of the large class of romantic stories that took their present form in the fourteenth century, though it can scarcely be questioned that something of them must have existed in some guise

at a much earlier date. Though the Frithiof
Saga is not mentioned in any earlier work, it
bears in one part signs of its having had an
earlier form: for some of the (apparent) prose
of it is really verse; and it is remarkable that
this happens in the typical part of the tale,
viz. where Frithiof comes disguised to King
Ring.

The *Viglund*, again, in spite of its story being
localised definitely enough, is confessedly nothing
but a pure fiction, and in more than one place
the tale-teller has borrowed from earlier stories:
e.g. the incident at p. 192 from the Frithiof;
and the fight in which the sons of Holmkell are
slain from the story of Helgi and Grim, the
sons of Droplaug. It should be mentioned that
the melody given in it is an old traditional one
in Iceland, and may be taken as an example of
the sort of tune to which the staves of verse in
the Sagas were sung.

The story of *Hogni and Hedinn* is a late and
amplified version of the mythological tale given
in the *Skáldskaparmál* (or Treatise on Poetic
Diction), a translation of which we add in a
note.

Roi the Fool, in spite of its very characteristic
Northern colouring, is a version of an Eastern

story, and is probably adapted directly from some
Latin translation of the mediæval Greek Syntipas,
the earliest European version of the "Seven
Wise Masters," which is also found in the
Thousand and One Nights under the title of "The
King, his Son, and the Seven Wezeers:" at
p. 163 of the 3rd vol. of Mr. Lane's translation
the reader will find the Arabian version of Roi
the Fool.[1]

The short tale of *Thorstein Staff-smitten* is a
kind of hanger-on to the more important story
of "the Weapon-firth Men," the people of a
district in the North-east of Iceland.   Biarni of
Hof is the hero of the second generation in this
tale: at the fight at Bodvarsdale, mentioned
more than once in our story, he met and de-
feated his cousin, whom he afterwards treated
with a generosity and forbearance much of a piece
with his dealings with Thorstein Staff-smitten.

[1] We must note here, in illustration of the wanderings of this story,
that it is found only in the ancient Icelandic MS. commonly called
the *Flateyjarbók*, and in that part of it which was written before 1380:
from the manner of its adaptation it would seem that the tale came to
Iceland from Denmark.   It is to be added, that the *Flateyjarbók* was
certainly written at Viðidalstungu (in Iceland) by two clerks, Jón
Þorhallson and Magnús Þorðarson, probably chaplains (*heimilis-
prestar*) of the lord of the manor, and belonged apparently from the
beginning to Jón Hákonarson, who by a charter (*máldagi*) for the
church of Viðidalstungu, dated 1394, is proved to have been master
of that stead about the time when the MS. was being written.

CHRONOLOGY

IN THE STORY OF GUNNLAUG THE WORM-TONGUE

<table>
<tr><td>Helga the Fair born . . . . circa</td><td>985</td></tr>
<tr><td>Gunnlaug Worm-tongue born . . . .</td><td>983</td></tr>
<tr><td>Gunnlaug attempts to run away . . .</td><td>998</td></tr>
<tr><td>Gunnlaug resides alternately at Burg and Gilsbank for three years . . . .</td><td>998–1001</td></tr>
<tr><td>Gunnlaug goes to Earl Eric of Hladir . .</td><td>1001</td></tr>
<tr><td>Gunnlaug goes to King Sigtrygg in Ireland, Earl Sigurd in Orkney, and Earl Sigurd of Skarir in Sweden . . . . . .</td><td>1002</td></tr>
<tr><td>Gunnlaug goes to King Olaf of Sweden . .</td><td>1003</td></tr>
<tr><td>Raven goes to Iceland . . . . .</td><td>1003</td></tr>
<tr><td>Gunnlaug goes to King Ethelred of England, and remains with him . . . .</td><td>1004–5</td></tr>
</table>

OBSERVE.—On p. 42 it is stated that in those days Knut the Great ruled in Denmark, &c. This is a mistake on the part of the writer of the Saga, as King Swein lived until A.D. 1014, when Knut succeeded to his throne; but it affects the chronology of the Saga in nowise.

<table>
<tr><td>Gunnlaug sails to Iceland in the autumn . .</td><td>1005</td></tr>
<tr><td>Gunnlaug fights a duel with Raven . . .</td><td>1006</td></tr>
<tr><td>Duels forbidden by law . . . . .</td><td>1006</td></tr>
<tr><td>Gunnlaug and Raven go abroad . . .</td><td>1006</td></tr>
<tr><td>Gunnlaug remains in Orkney . . . .</td><td>1007</td></tr>
<tr><td>Raven sojourns in Thrandheim . . . .</td><td>1007</td></tr>
<tr><td>Gunnlaug spends the winter with Earl Eric .</td><td>1008</td></tr>
<tr><td>Gunnlaug falls, 23 years of age . . . .</td><td>1008</td></tr>
</table>

CONTENTS

THE STORY OF

GUNNLAUG THE WORM-TONGUE
AND RAVEN THE SKALD

THE STORY OF

GUNNLAUG THE WORM-TONGUE
AND RAVEN THE SKALD

EVEN AS ARI THORGILSON THE LEARNED, THE PRIEST,
HATH TOLD IT, WHO WAS THE MAN OF ALL ICELAND
MOST LEARNED IN TALES OF THE LAND'S INHABITING
AND IN LORE OF TIME AGONE

CHAPTER I

OF THORSTEIN EGILSON AND HIS KIN

THERE was a man called Thorstein, the son
of Egil, the son of Skallagrim, the son of
Kveldulf the Hersir of Norway. Asgerd was the
mother of Thorstein; she was the daughter of
Biorn Hold. Thorstein dwelt at Burg in Burg-
firth; he was rich of fee, and a great chief, a
wise man, meek and of measure in all wise. He
was nought of such wondrous growth and strength
as his father Egil had been; yet was he a right
mighty man, and much beloved of all folk.

Thorstein was goodly to look on, flaxen-haired,
and the best-eyed of men; and so say men of
lore that many of the kin of the Mere-men, who

are come of Egil, have been the goodliest folk;
yet, for all that, this kindred have differed much
herein, for it is said that some of them have been
accounted the most ill-favoured of men: but in
that kin have been also many men of great prowess in many wise, such as Kiartan, the son of
Olaf Peacock, and Slaying-Bardi, and Skuli, the
son of Thorstein. Some have been great bards,
too, in that kin, as Biorn, the champion of Hit-
dale, priest Einar Skulison, Snorri Sturluson, and
many others.

Now, Thorstein had to wife Jofrid, the daughter of Gunnar, the son of Hlifar. This Gunnar
was the best skilled in weapons, and the lithest
of limb of all bonder-folk who have been in
Iceland; the second was Gunnar of Lithend; but
Steinthor of Ere was the third. Jofrid was
eighteen winters old when Thorstein wedded her;
she was a widow, for Thorodd, son of Odd of
Tongue, had had her to wife aforetime. Their
daughter was Hungerd, who was brought up at
Thorstein's at Burg. Jofrid was a very stirring
woman; she and Thorstein had many children
betwixt them, but few of them come into this
tale. Skuli was the eldest of their sons, Kollsvein
the second, Egil the third.

CHAPTER II

OF THORSTEIN'S DREAM

ONE summer, it is said, a ship came from over the main into Gufaros. Bergfinn was he hight who was the master thereof, a Northman of kin, rich in goods, and somewhat stricken in years, and a wise man he was withal.

Now, goodman Thorstein rode to the ship, as it was his wont mostly to rule the market, and this he did now. The Eastmen got housed, but Thorstein took the master to himself, for thither he prayed to go. Bergfinn was of few words throughout the winter, but Thorstein treated him well. The Eastman had great joy of dreams.

One day in spring-tide Thorstein asked Bergfinn if he would ride with him up to Hawkfell, where at that time was the Thing-stead of the Burg-firthers; for Thorstein had been told that the walls of his booth had fallen in. The Eastman said he had good will to go, so that day they rode, some three together, from home, and the house-carles of Thorstein withal, till they came up under Hawkfell to a farmstead called Foxholes. There dwelt a man of small wealth called Atli, who was Thorstein's tenant. Thorstein bade him come and work with them, and bring with him hoe and spade. This he did, and when they came to the tofts of the booth, they set to work all of them, and did out the walls.

The weather was hot with sunshine that day, and Thorstein and the Eastman grew heavy; and when they had moved out the walls, those two sat down within the tofts, and Thorstein slept, and fared ill in his sleep. The Eastman sat beside him, and let him have his dream fully out, and when he awoke he was much wearied. Then the Eastman asked him what he had dreamt, as he had had such an ill time of it in his sleep.

Thorstein said, "Nay, dreams betoken nought."

But as they rode homeward in the evening, the Eastman asked him again what he had dreamt.

Thorstein said, "If I tell thee the dream, then shalt thou unriddle it to me, as it verily is."

The Eastman said he would risk it.

Then Thorstein said: "This was my dream; for methought I was at home at Burg, standing outside the men's-door, and I looked up at the house-roof, and on the ridge I saw a swan, goodly and fair, and I thought it was mine own, and deemed it good beyond all things. Then I saw a great eagle sweep down from the mountains, and fly thitherward and alight beside the swan, and chuckle over her lovingly; and methought the swan seemed well content thereat; but I noted that the eagle was black-eyed, and that on him were iron claws: valiant he seemed to me.

"After this I thought I saw another fowl come

flying from the south quarter, and he, too, came hither to Burg, and sat down on the house beside the swan, and would fain be fond with her. This also was a mighty eagle.

"But soon I thought that the eagle first-come ruffled up at the coming of the other. Then they fought fiercely and long, and, this I saw that both bled, and such was the end of their play, that each tumbled either way down from the house-roof, and there they lay both dead.

"But the swan sat left alone, drooping much, and sad of semblance.

"Then I saw a fowl fly from the west; that was a falcon, and he sat beside the swan and made fondly towards her, and they flew away both together into one and the same quarter, and therewith I awoke.

"But a dream of no mark this is," he says, "and will in all likelihood betoken gales, that they shall meet in the air from those quarters whence I deemed the fowl flew."

The Eastman spake: "I deem it nowise such," saith he.

Thorstein said, "Make of the dream, then, what seemeth likest to thee, and let me hear."

Then said the Eastman: "These birds are like to be fetches of men: but thy wife sickens now, and she will give birth to a woman-child fair and lovely; and dearly thou wilt love her; but high-born men shall woo thy daughter, coming from such quarters as the eagles seemed to fly from, and shall love her with overweening love, and

shall fight about her, and both lose their lives
thereby.   And thereafter a third man, from the
quarter whence came the falcon, shall woo her,
and to that man shall she be wedded.   Now, I
have unravelled thy dream, and I think things
will befall as I have said."

Thorstein answered : " In evil and unfriendly
wise is the dream interpreted, nor do I deem thee
fit for the work of unriddling dreams."

The Eastman said, " Thou shalt find how it
will come to pass."

But Thorstein estranged himself from the Eastman thenceforward, and he left that summer,
and now he is out of the tale.

CHAPTER III

OF THE BIRTH AND FOSTERING OF HELGA THE FAIR

THIS summer Thorstein got ready to ride to the Thing, and spake to Jofrid his wife before he went from home. "So is it," he says, "that thou art with child now, but thy child shall be cast forth if thou bear a woman; but nourished if it be a man."

Now, at this time when all the land was heathen, it was somewhat the wont of such men as had little wealth, and were like to have many young children on their hands, to have them cast forth, but an evil deed it was always deemed to be.

And now, when Thorstein had said this, Jofrid answers, "This is a word all unlike thee, such a man as thou art, and surely to a wealthy man like thee it will not seem good that this should be done."

Thorstein answered: "Thou knowest my mind, and that no good will hap if my will be thwarted."

So he rode to the Thing; but while he was gone Jofrid gave birth to a woman-child wondrous fair. The women would fain show her to the mother; she said there was little need thereof, but had her shepherd Thorvard called to her, and spake to him :—

"Thou shalt take my horse and saddle it, and bring this child west to Herdholt, to Thorgerd, Egil's daughter, and pray her to nourish it secretly, so that Thorstein may not know thereof. For with such looks of love do I behold this child, that surely I cannot bear to have it cast forth. Here are three marks of silver, have them in reward of thy work ; but west there Thorgerd will get thee fare and food over the sea."

Then Thorvard did her bidding ; he rode with the child to Herdholt, and gave it into Thorgerd's hands, and she had it nourished at a tenant's of hers who dwelt at Freedmans-stead up in Hvamfirth ; but she got fare for Thorvard north in Steingrims-firth, in Shell-creek, and gave him meet outfit for his sea-faring : he went thence abroad, and is now out of the story.

Now when Thorstein came home from the Thing, Jofrid told him that the child had been cast forth according to his word, but that the herdsman had fled away and stolen her horse. Thorstein said she had done well, and got himself another herdsman. So six winters passed, and this matter was nowise wotted of.

Now in those days Thorstein rode to Herdholt, being bidden there as guest of his brother-in-law, Olaf Peacock, the son of Hoskuld, who was then deemed to be the chief highest of worth among all men west there. Good cheer was made Thorstein, as was like to be ; and one day at the feast it is said that Thorgerd sat in the high seat talking with her brother Thorstein, while Olaf was talking to other men; but on the bench right over against them sat three little maidens.   Then said Thorgerd,—

"How dost thou, brother, like the look of these three little maidens sitting straight before us?"

"Right well," he answers, "but one is by far the fairest; she has all the goodliness of Olaf, but the whiteness and the countenance of us, the Mere-men."

Thorgerd answered: "Surely this is true, brother, wherein thou sayest that she has the fairness and countenance of us Mere-folk, but the goodliness of Olaf Peacock she has not got, for she is not his daughter."

"How can that be," says Thorstein, "being thy daughter none the less?"

She answered: "To say sooth, kinsman," quoth she, "this fair maiden is not my daughter, but thine."

And therewith she told him all as it had befallen, and prayed him to forgive her and his own wife that trespass.

Thorstein said: "I cannot blame you two for having done this; most things will fall as they are fated, and well have ye covered over my folly: so look I on this maiden that I deem it great good luck to have so fair a child.   But now, what is her name?"

"Helga she is called," says Thorgerd.

" Helga the Fair," says Thorstein. " But now shalt thou make her ready to come home with me."

She did so, and Thorstein was led out with good gifts, and Helga rode with him to his home, and was brought up there with much honour and great love from father and mother and all her kin.

CHAPTER IV

OF GUNNLAUG WORM-TONGUE AND HIS KIN

NOW at this time there dwelt at Gilsbank, up in White-water-side, Illugi the Black, son of Hallkel, the son of Hrosskel. The mother of Illugi was Thurid Dandle, daughter of Gunnlaug Worm-tongue.

Illugi was the next greatest chief in Burg-firth after Thorstein Egilson. He was a man of broad lands and hardy of mood, and wont to do well to his friends ; he had to wife Ingibiorg, the daughter of Asbiorn Hordson, from Ornolfsdale ; the mother of Ingibiorg was Thorgerd, the daughter of Midfirth-Skeggi. The children of Illugi and Ingibiorg were many, but few of them have to do with this story. Hermund was one of their sons, and Gunnlaug another ; both were hopeful men, and at this time of ripe growth.

It is told of Gunnlaug that he was quick of growth in his early youth, big, and strong ; his hair was light red, and very goodly of fashion ; he was dark-eyed, somewhat ugly-nosed, yet of lovesome countenance ; thin of flank he was, and broad of shoulder, and the best-wrought of men ; his whole mind was very masterful ; eager was he from his youth up, and in all wise unsparing and hardy; he was a great skald, but somewhat bitter in his rhyming, and therefore was he called Gunnlaug Worm-tongue.

Hermund was the best beloved of the two brothers, and had the mien of a great man.

When Gunnlaug was fifteen winters old he prayed his father for goods to fare abroad withal, and said he had will to travel and see the manners of other folk. Master Illugi was slow to take the matter up, and said he was unlike to be deemed good in the out-lands " when I can scarcely shape thee to my own liking at home."

On a morning but a very little afterwards it happened that Illugi came out early, and saw that his storehouse was opened, and that some sacks of wares, six of them, had been brought out into the road, and therewithal too some pack-gear. Now, as he wondered at this, there came up a man leading four horses, and who should it be but his son Gunnlaug. Then said he :—

" I it was who brought out the sacks."

Illugi asked him why he had done so. He said that they should make his faring goods.

Illugi said : " In nowise shalt thou thwart my will, nor fare anywhere sooner than I like ! " and in again he swung the ware-sacks therewith.

Then Gunnlaug rode thence and came in the evening down to Burg, and goodman Thorstein asked him to bide there, and Gunnlaug was fain of that proffer. He told Thorstein how things had gone betwixt him and his father, and Thorstein offered to let him bide there as long as he liked, and for some seasons Gunnlaug abode there, and learned law-craft of Thorstein, and all men accounted well of him.

Now Gunnlaug and Helga would be always at the chess-playing together, and very soon each found favour with the other, as came to be proven well enough afterwards : they were very nigh of an age.

Helga was so fair, that men of lore say that she was the fairest woman of Iceland, then or since ; her hair was so plenteous and long that it could cover her all over, and it was as fair as a band of gold ; nor was there any so good to choose as Helga the Fair in all Burgfirth, and far and wide elsewhere.

Now one day, as men sat in the hall at Burg, Gunnlaug spake to Thorstein : "One thing in law there is which thou hast not taught me, and that is how to woo me a wife."

Thorstein said, " That is but a small matter," and therewith taught him how to go about it.

Then said Gunnlaug, " Now shalt thou try if I have understood all : I shall take thee by the hand and make as if I were wooing thy daughter Helga."

" I see no need of that," says Thorstein. Gunnlaug, however, groped then and there after his hand, and seizing it said, " Nay, grant me this though."

" Do as thou wilt, then," said Thorstein ; " but be it known to all who are hereby that this shall be as if it had been unspoken, nor shall any guile follow herein."

Then Gunnlaug named for himself witnesses, and betrothed Helga to him, and asked thereafter if it would stand good thus. Thorstein said that it was well; and those who were present were mightily pleased at all this.

CHAPTER V

OF RAVEN AND HIS KIN

THERE was a man called Onund, who dwelt in the south at Mossfell : he was the wealthiest of men, and had a priesthood south there about the nesses.   He was married, and his wife was called Geirny.   She was the daughter of Gnup, son of Mold-Gnup, who settled at Grindwick, in the south country.   Their sons were Raven, and Thorarin, and Eindridi ; they were all hopeful men, but Raven was in all wise the first of them.   He was a big man and a strong, the sightliest of men and a good skald ; and when he was fully grown he fared between sundry lands, and was well accounted of wherever he came.

Thorod the Sage, the son of Eyvind, then dwelt at Hjalli, south in Olfus, with Skapti his son, who was then the spokesman-at-law in Iceland.   The mother of Skapti was Ranveig, daughter of Gnup, the son of Mold-Gnup ; and Skapti and the sons of Onund were sisters' sons. Between these kinsmen was much friendship as well as kinship.

At this time Thorfin, the son of Selthorir, dwelt at Red-Mel, and had seven sons, who were all the

B

hopefullest of men; and of them were these—
Thorgils, Eyjolf, and Thorir; and they were all
the greatest men out there.

But these men who have now been named lived
all at one and the same time.

Next to this befell those tidings, the best that
ever have befallen here in Iceland, that the whole
land became Christian, and that all folk cast off
the old faith.

CHAPTER VI

HOW HELGA WAS VOWED TO GUNNLAUG, AND OF GUNNLAUG'S FARING ABROAD

GUNNLAUG WORM-TONGUE was, as is aforesaid, whiles at Burg with Thorstein, whiles with his father Illugi at Gilsbank, three winters together, and was by now eighteen winters old ; and father and son were now much more of a mind.

There was a man called Thorkel the Black ; he was a house-carle of Illugi, and near akin to him, and had been brought up in his house. To him fell an heritage north at As, in Water-dale, and he prayed Gunnlaug to go with him thither. This he did, and so they rode, the two together, to As. There they got the fee ; it was given up to them by those who had the keeping of it, mostly because of Gunnlaug's furtherance.

But as they rode from the north they guested at Grimstongue, at a rich bonder's who dwelt there ; but in the morning a herdsman took Gunnlaug's horse, and it had sweated much by then he got it back. Then Gunnlaug smote the herdsman, and stunned him ; but the bonder would in nowise bear this, and claimed boot

therefor.   Gunnlaug offered to pay him one
mark.   The bonder thought it too little.

Then Gunnlaug sang—

> " Bade I the middling mighty
> To have a mark of waves' flame ;
> Giver of grey seas' glitter,
> This gift shalt thou make shift with.
> If the elf-sun of the waters
> From out of purse thou lettest,
> O waster of the worm's bed,
> Awaits thee sorrow later."

So the peace was made as Gunnlaug bade, and
in such wise the two rode south.

Now, a little while after, Gunnlaug asked his
father a second time for goods for going abroad.

Illugi says, " Now shalt thou have thy will, for
thou hast wrought thyself into something better
than thou wert." So Illugi rode hastily from
home, and bought for Gunnlaug half a ship
which lay in Gufaros, from Audun Festargram—
this Audun was he who would not flit abroad
the sons of Oswif the Wise, after the slaying of
Kiartan Olafson, as is told in the story of the
Laxdalemen, which thing though betid later than
this.—And when Illugi came home Gunnlaug
thanked him well.

Thorkel the Black betook himself to seafaring
with Gunnlaug, and their wares were brought to
the ship ; but Gunnlaug was at Burg while they
made her ready, and found more cheer in talk
with Helga than in toiling with chapmen.

Now one day Thorstein asked Gunnlaug if he

would ride to his horses with him up to Long-water-dale. Gunnlaug said he would. So they ride both together till they come to the mountain-dairies of Thorstein, called Thorgilsstead. There were stud-horses of Thorstein, four of them together, all red of hue. There was one horse very goodly, but little tried: this horse Thorstein offered to give to Gunnlaug. He said he was in no need of horses, as he was going away from the country; and so they ride to other stud-horses. There was a grey horse with four mares, and he was the best of horses in Burgfirth. This one, too, Thorstein offered to give Gunnlaug, but he said, "I desire these in no wise more than the others; but why dost thou not bid me what I will take?"

"What is that?" said Thorstein.

"Helga the Fair, thy daughter," says Gunnlaug.

"That rede is not to be settled so hastily," said Thorstein; and therewithal got on other talk. And now they ride homewards down along Long-water.

Then said Gunnlaug, "I must needs know what thou wilt answer me about the wooing."

Thorstein answers: "I need not thy vain talk," says he.

Gunnlaug says, "This is my whole mind, and no vain words."

Thorstein says, "Thou shouldst first know thine own will. Art thou not bound to fare abroad? and yet thou makest as if thou wouldst go marry. Neither art thou an even match for Helga while thou art so unsettled, and therefore this cannot so much as be looked at."

Gunnlaug says, "Where lookest thou for a match for thy daughter, if thou wilt not give her to the son of Illugi the Black; or who are they throughout Burg-firth who are of more note than he?"

Thorstein answered: "I will not play at men-mating," says he, "but if thou wert such a man as he is, thou wouldst not be turned away."

Gunnlaug said, "To whom wilt thou give thy daughter rather than to me?"

Said Thorstein, "Hereabout are many good men to choose from. Thorfin of Red-Mel hath seven sons, and all of them men of good manners."

Gunnlaug answers, "Neither Onund nor Thorfin are men as good as my father. Nay, thou thyself clearly fallest short of him—or what hast thou to set against his strife with Thorgrim the Priest, the son of Kiallak, and his sons, at Thorsness Thing, where he carried all that was in debate?"

Thorstein answers, "I drave away Steinar, the son of Onund Sioni, which was deemed some-what of a deed."

Gunnlaug says, "Therein thou wast holpen by thy father Egil; and, to end all, it is for few bonders to cast away my alliance."

Said Thorstein, "Carry thy cowing away to the fellows up yonder at the mountains; for down here, on the Meres, it shall avail thee nought."

Now in the evening they come home; but next morning Gunnlaug rode up to Gilsbank, and prayed his father to ride with him a-wooing out to Burg.

Illugi answered, "Thou art an unsettled man, being bound for faring abroad, but makest now as if thou wouldst busy thyself with wife-wooing; and so much do I know, that this is not to Thorstein's mind."

Gunnlaug answers, "I shall go abroad all the same, nor shall I be well pleased but if thou further this."

So after this Illugi rode with eleven men from home down to Burg, and Thorstein greeted him well.   Early in the morning Illugi said to Thorstein, "I would speak to thee."

"Let us go, then, to the top of the Burg, and talk together there," said Thorstein; and so they did, and Gunnlaug went with them.

Then said Illugi, "My kinsman Gunnlaug tells me that he has begun a talk with thee on his own behalf, praying that he might woo thy daughter Helga; but now I would fain know what is like to come of this matter.   His kin is known to thee, and our possessions; from my hand shall be spared neither land nor rule over men, if such things might perchance further matters."

Thorstein said, "Herein alone Gunnlaug pleases me not, that I find him an unsettled man; but if he were of a mind like thine, little would I hang back."

Illugi said, "It will cut our friendship across if thou gainsayest me and my son an equal match."

Thorstein answers, "For thy words and our friendship then, Helga shall be vowed, but not betrothed, to Gunnlaug, and shall bide for him three winters : but Gunnlaug shall go abroad and shape himself to the ways of good men; but I shall be free from all these matters if he does not then come back, or if his ways are not to my liking."

Thereat they parted; Illugi rode home, but Gunnlaug rode to his ship. But when they had wind at will they sailed for the main, and made the northern part of Norway, and sailed landward along Thrandheim to Nidaros; there they rode in the harbour, and unshipped their goods.

CHAPTER VII

OF GUNNLAUG IN THE EAST AND THE WEST

IN those days Earl Eric, the son of Hakon, and his brother Svein, ruled in Norway. Earl Eric abode as then at Hladir, which was left to him by his father, and a mighty lord he was. Skuli, the son of Thorstein, was with the earl at that time, and was one of his court, and well esteemed.

Now they say that Gunnlaug and Audun Festargram, and seven of them together, went up to Hladir to the earl. Gunnlaug was so clad that he had on a grey kirtle and white long-hose; he had a boil on his foot by the instep, and from this oozed blood and matter as he strode on. In this guise he went before the earl with Audun and the rest of them, and greeted him well. The earl knew Audun, and asked him tidings from Iceland. Audun told him what there was toward. Then the earl asked Gunnlaug who he was, and Gunnlaug told him his name and kin. Then the earl said : "Skuli Thorstein's son, what manner of man is this in Iceland?"

"Lord," says he, "give him good welcome, for he is the son of the best man in Iceland, Illugi the Black of Gilsbank, and my foster-brother withal."

The earl asked, "What ails thy foot, Icelander?"

"A boil, lord," said he.

"And yet thou wentest not halt."

Gunnlaug answers, "Why go halt while both legs are long alike?"

Then said one of the earl's men, called Thorir: "He swaggereth hugely, this Icelander! It would not be amiss to try him a little."

Gunnlaug looked at him and sang—

> "A courtman there is
> Full evil I wis,
> A bad man and black,
> Belief let him lack."

Then would Thorir seize an axe. The earl spake: "Let it be," says he; "to such things men should pay no heed. But now, Icelander, how old a man art thou?"

Gunnlaug answers: "I am eighteen winters old as now," says he.

Then says Earl Eric, "My spell is that thou shalt not live eighteen winters more."

Gunnlaug said, somewhat under his breath: "Pray not against me, but for thyself rather."

The earl asked thereat, "What didst thou say, Icelander?"

Gunnlaug answers, "What I thought well befitting, that thou shouldst bid no prayers against me, but pray well for thyself rather."

"What prayers, then?" says the earl.

"That thou mightest not meet thy death after the manner of Earl Hakon, thy father."

The earl turned red as blood, and bade them take the rascal in haste; but Skuli stepped up to the earl, and said: "Do this for my words, lord, and give this man peace, so that he depart at his swiftest."

The earl answered, "At his swiftest let him be off then, if he will have peace, and never let him come again within my realm."

Then Skuli went out with Gunnlaug down to the bridges, where there was an England-bound ship ready to put out; therein Skuli got for Gunnlaug a berth, as well as for Thorkel, his kinsman; but Gunnlaug gave his ship into Audun's ward, and so much of his goods as he did not take with him.

Now sail Gunnlaug and his fellows into the English main, and come at autumntide south to London Bridge, where they hauled ashore their ship.

Now at that time King Ethelred, the son of Edgar, ruled over England, and was a good lord; this winter he sat in London. But in those days there was the same tongue in England as in Norway and Denmark; but the tongues changed when William the Bastard won England, for thenceforward French went current there, for he was of French kin.

Gunnlaug went presently to the king, and greeted him well and worthily. The king asked him from what land he came, and Gunnlaug told him all as it was. " But," said he, " I have come to meet thee, lord, for that I have made a song on thee, and I would that it might please thee to hearken to that song." The king said it should be so, and Gunnlaug gave forth the song well and proudly; and this is the burden thereof :—

> " As God are all folk fearing
> The free lord King of England,
> Kin of all kings and all folk,
> To Ethelred the head bow."

The king thanked him for the song, and gave him as song-reward a scarlet cloak lined with the costliest of furs, and golden-broidered down to the hem ; and made him his man ; and Gunnlaug was with him all the winter, and was well accounted of.

One day, in the morning early, Gunnlaug met three men in a certain street, and Thororm was the name of their leader ; he was big and strong, and right evil to deal with. He said, " Northman, lend me some money."

Gunnlaug answered, " That were ill counselled to lend one's money to unknown men."

He said, " I will pay it thee back on a named day."

" Then shall it be risked," says Gunnlaug ; and he lent him the fee withal.

But some time afterwards Gunnlaug met the king, and told him of the money-lending. The king answered, " Now hast thou thriven little, for this is the greatest robber and reiver; deal with him in no wise, but I will give thee money as much as thine was."

Gunnlaug said, "Then do we, your men, do after a sorry sort, if, treading sackless folk under foot, we let such fellows as this deal us out our lot. Nay, that shall never be."

Soon after he met Thororm and claimed the fee of him. He said he was not going to pay it.

Then sang Gunnlaug :—

> " Evil counselled art thou,
>   Gold from us withholding;
>   The reddener of the edges,
>   Pricking on with tricking.
>   Wot ye what? they called me,
>   Worm-tongue, yet a youngling;
>   Nor for nought so hight I;
>   Now is time to show it!"

"Now I will make an offer good in law," says Gunnlaug; "that thou either pay me my money, or else that thou go on holm with me in three nights' space."

Then laughed the viking, and said, "Before thee none have come to that, to call me to holm, despite of all the ruin that many a man has had to take at my hands. Well, I am ready to go."

Thereon they parted for that time.

Gunnlaug told the king what had befallen; and he said, "Now, indeed, have things taken a right hopeless turn; for this man's eyes can dull any weapon. But thou shalt follow my rede; here is a sword I will give thee—with that thou shalt fight, but before the battle show him another."

Gunnlaug thanked the king well therefor.

Now when they were ready for the holm, Thororm asked what sort of a sword it was that he had. Gunnlaug unsheathed it and showed him, but had a loop round the handle of the king's sword, and slipped it over his hand; the bearserk looked on the sword, and said, "I fear not that sword."

But now he dealt a blow on Gunnlaug with his sword, and cut off from him nigh all his shield; Gunnlaug smote in turn with the king's gift; the bearserk stood shieldless before him, thinking he had the same weapon he had shown him, but Gunnlaug smote him his deathblow then and there.

The king thanked him for his work, and he got much fame therefor, both in England and far and wide elsewhere.

In the spring, when ships sailed from land to land, Gunnlaug prayed King Ethelred for leave to sail somewhither; the king asks what he was about then. Gunnlaug said, "I would fulfil what I have given my word to do," and sang this stave withal :—

> " My ways must I be wending
> Three kings' walls to see yet,
> And carls twain, as I promised
> Erewhile to land-sharers.
> Neither will I wend me
> Back, the worms'-bed lacking,
> By war-lord's son, the wealth-free,
> For work done gift well given."

"So be it, then, skald," said the king, and withal he gave him a ring that weighed six ounces; "but," said he, "thou shalt give me thy word to come back next autumn, for I will not let thee go altogether, because of thy great prowess."

CHAPTER VIII

OF GUNNLAUG IN IRELAND

THEREAFTER Gunnlaug sailed from England with chapmen north to Dublin. In those days King Sigtrygg Silky-beard, son of King Olaf Kvaran and Queen Kormlada, ruled over Ireland; and he had then borne sway but a little while. Gunnlaug went before the king, and greeted him well and worthily. The king received him as was meet. Then Gunnlaug said, "I have made a song on thee, and I would fain have silence therefor."

The king answered, "No men have before now come forward with songs for me, and surely will I hearken to thine." Then Gunnlaug brought the song, whereof this is the burden :—

> "Swaru's steed
> Doth Sigtrygg feed."

And this is therein also :—

> "Praise-worth I can
> Well measure in man,
> And kings, one by one—
> Lo here, Kvaran's son !
> Grudgeth the king
> Gift of gold ring ?

I, singer, know
His wont to bestow.
Let the high king say,
Heard he or this day,
Song drapu-measure
Dearer a treasure."

The king thanked him for the song, and called his treasurer to him, and said, " How shall the song be rewarded ? "

" What hast thou will to give, lord ? " says he.

" How will it be rewarded if I give him two ships for it ? " said the king.

Then said the treasurer, " This is too much, lord ; other kings give in reward of songs good keepsakes, fair swords, or golden rings."

So the king gave him his own raiment of new scarlet, a gold-embroidered kirtle, and a cloak lined with choice furs, and a gold ring which weighed a mark. Gunnlaug thanked him well.

He dwelt a short time here, and then went thence to the Orkneys.

Then was lord in Orkney, Earl Sigurd, the son of Hlodver : he was friendly to Icelanders. Now Gunnlaug greeted the earl well, and said he had a song to bring him. The earl said he would listen thereto, since he was of such great kin in Iceland.

Then Gunnlaug brought the song ; it was a shorter lay, and well done. The earl gave him for lay-reward a broad axe, all inlaid with silver, and bade him abide with him.

Gunnlaug thanked him both for his gift and

C

his offer, but said he was bound east for Sweden ; and thereafter he went on board ship with chapmen who sailed to Norway.

In the autumn they came east to King's Cliff, Thorkel, his kinsman, being with him all the time. From King's Cliff they got a guide up to West Gothland, and came upon a cheaping-stead, called Skarir : there ruled an earl called Sigurd, a man stricken in years. Gunnlaug went before him, and told him he had made a song on him ; the earl gave a willing ear hereto, and Gunnlaug brought the song, which was a shorter lay.

The earl thanked him, and rewarded the song well, and bade him abide there that winter.

Earl Sigurd had a great Yule-feast in the winter, and on Yule-eve came thither men sent from Earl Eric of Norway, twelve of them together, and brought gifts to Earl Sigurd. The earl made them good cheer, and bade them sit by Gunnlaug through the Yule-tide ; and there was great mirth at drinks.

Now the Gothlanders said that no earl was greater or of more fame than Earl Sigurd ; but the Norwegians thought that Earl Eric was by far the foremost of the two. Hereon would they bandy words, till they both took Gunnlaug to be umpire in the matter.

Then he sang this stave :—

> " Tell ye, staves of spear-din,
> How on sleek-side sea-horse
> Oft this earl hath proven
> Over-toppling billows ;

> But Eric, victory's ash-tree,
> Oft hath seen in east-seas
> More of high blue billows
> Before the bows a-roaring."

Both sides were content with his finding, but the Norwegians the best. But after Yule-tide those messengers left with gifts of goodly things, which Earl Sigurd sent to Earl Eric.

Now they told Earl Eric of Gunnlaug's finding: the earl thought that he had shown upright dealing and friendship to him herein, and let out some words, saying that Gunnlaug should have good peace throughout his land. What the earl had said came thereafter to the ears of Gunnlaug.

But now Earl Sigurd gave Gunnlaug a guide east to Tenthland, in Sweden, as he had asked.

CHAPTER IX

OF THE QUARREL BETWEEN GUNNLAUG AND
RAVEN BEFORE THE SWEDISH KING

IN those days King Olaf the Swede, son of King
Eric the Victorious, and Sigrid the High-
counselled, daughter of Skogul Tosti, ruled over
Sweden. He was a mighty king and renowned,
and full fain of fame.

Gunnlaug came to Upsala towards the time of
the Thing of the Swedes in spring-tide ; and when
he got to see the king, he greeted him. The
king took his greeting well, and asked who he
was. He said he was an Iceland-man.

Then the king called out : " Raven," says he,
" what man is he in Iceland ? "

Then one stood up from the lower bench, a
big man and a stalwart, and stepped up before
the king, and spake : " Lord," says he, " he is
of good kin, and himself the most stalwart of
men."

" Let him go, then, and sit beside thee," said
the king.

Then Gunnlaug said, " I have a song to set
forth before thee, king, and I would fain have
peace while thou hearkenest thereto."

"Go ye first, and sit ye down," says the king, "for there is no leisure now to sit listening to songs."

So they did as he bade them.

Now Gunnlaug and Raven fell a-talking together, and each told each of his travels. Raven said that he had gone the summer before from Iceland to Norway, and had come east to Sweden in the forepart of winter. They soon got friendly together.

But one day, when the Thing was over, they were both before the king, Gunnlaug and Raven.

Then spake Gunnlaug, "Now, lord, I would that thou shouldst hear the song."

"That I may do now," said the king.

"My song too will I set forth now," says Raven.

"Thou mayst do so," said the king.

Then Gunnlaug said, "I will set forth mine first if thou wilt have it so, king."

"Nay," said Raven, "it behoveth me to be first, lord, for I myself came first to thee."

"Whereto came our fathers forth, so that my father was the little boat towed behind? Whereto, but nowhere?" says Gunnlaug. "And in likewise shall it be with us."

Raven answered, "Let us be courteous enough not to make this a matter of bandying of words. Let the king rule here."

The king said, "Let Gunnlaug set forth his song first, for he will not be at peace till he has his will."

Then Gunnlaug set forth the song which he had made to King Olaf, and when it was at an end the king spake. "Raven," says he, "how is the song done?"

"Right well," he answered; "it is a song full of big words and little beauty; a somewhat rugged song, as is Gunnlaug's own mood."

"Well, Raven, thy song," said the king.

Raven gave it forth, and when it was done the king said, "How is this song made, Gunnlaug?"

"Well it is, lord," he said; "this is a pretty song, as is Raven himself to behold, and delicate of countenance. But why didst thou make a short song on the king, Raven? Didst thou perchance deem him unworthy of a long one?"

Raven answered, "Let us not talk longer on this; matters will be taken up again, though it be later."

And thereat they parted.

Soon after Raven became a man of King Olaf's, and asked him leave to go away. This the king granted him. And when Raven was ready to go, he spake to Gunnlaug, and said, "Now shall our friendship be ended, for that thou must needs shame me here before great men; but in time to come I shall cast on thee no less shame than thou hadst will to cast on me here."

Gunnlaug answers: "Thy threats grieve me nought. Nowhere are we likely to come where I shall be thought less worthy than thou."

King Olaf gave to Raven good gifts at parting, and thereafter he went away.

CHAPTER X

HOW RAVEN CAME HOME TO ICELAND, AND ASKED FOR HELGA TO WIFE

NOW this spring Raven came from the east to Thrandheim, and fitted out his ship, and sailed in the summer to Iceland. He brought his ship to Leiruvag, below the Heath, and his friends and kinsmen were right fain of him. That winter he was at home with his father, but the summer after he met at the Althing his kinsman, Skapti the law-man.

Then said Raven to him, " Thine aid would I have to go a-wooing to Thorstein Egilson, to bid Helga his daughter."

Skapti answered, " But is she not already vowed to Gunnlaug Worm-tongue ? "

Said Raven, " Is not the appointed time of waiting between them passed by ? And far too wanton is he withal, that he should hold or heed it aught."

" Let us then do as thou wouldst," said Skapti.

Thereafter they went with many men to the booth of Thorstein Egilson, and he greeted them well.

Then Skapti spoke: " Raven, my kinsman, is minded to woo thy daughter Helga. Thou knowest well his blood, his wealth, and his good manners, his many mighty kinsmen and friends."

Thorstein said, " She is already the vowed maiden of Gunnlaug, and with him shall I hold all words spoken."

Skapti said, " Are not the three winters worn now that were named between you ? "

" Yes," said Thorstein ; " but the summer is not yet worn, and he may still come out this summer."

Then Skapti said, " But if he cometh not this summer, what hope may we have of the matter then ? "

Thorstein answered, " We are like to come here next summer, and then may we see what may wisely be done, but it will not do to speak hereof longer as at this time."

Thereon they parted. And men rode home from the Althing. But this talk of Raven's wooing of Helga was nought hidden.

That summer Gunnlaug came not out.

The next summer, at the Althing, Skapti and his folk pushed the wooing eagerly, and said that Thorstein was free as to all matters with Gunnlaug.

Thorstein answered, " I have few daughters to see to, and fain am I that they should not be the cause of strife to any man. Now I will first see Illugi the Black." And so he did.

And when they met, he said to Illugi, " Dost

thou not think that I am free from all troth with thy son Gunnlaug?"

Illugi said, "Surely, if thou willest it. Little can I say herein, as I do not know clearly what Gunnlaug is about."

Then Thorstein went to Skapti, and a bargain was struck that the wedding should be at Burg, about winter-nights, if Gunnlaug did not come out that summer; but that Thorstein should be free from all troth with Raven if Gunnlaug should come and fetch his bride.

After this men ride home from the Thing, and Gunnlaug's coming was long drawn out. But Helga thought evilly of all these redes.

CHAPTER XI

OF HOW GUNNLAUG MUST NEEDS ABIDE AWAY FROM ICELAND

NOW it is to be told of Gunnlaug that he went from Sweden the same summer that Raven went to Iceland, and good gifts he had from King Olaf at parting.

King Ethelred welcomed Gunnlaug worthily, and that winter he was with the king, and was held in great honour.

In those days Knut the Great, son of Svein, ruled Denmark, and had new-taken his father's heritage, and he vowed ever to wage war on England, for that his father had won a great realm there before he died west in that same land.

And at that time there was a great army of Danish men west there, whose chief was Heming, the son of Earl Strut-Harald, and brother to Earl Sigvaldi, and he held for King Knut that land that Svein had won.

Now in the spring Gunnlaug asked the king for leave to go away, but he said, "It ill beseems that thou, my man, shouldst go away now, when all bodes such mighty war in the land."

Gunnlaug said, "Thou shalt rule, lord; but

give me leave next summer to depart, if the Danes come not."

The king answered, " Then we shall see."

Now this summer went by, and the next winter, but no Danes came; and after midsummer Gunnlaug got his leave to depart from the king, and went thence east to Norway, and found Earl Eric in Thrandheim, at Hladir, and the earl greeted him well, and bade him abide with him. Gunnlaug thanked him for his offer, but said he would first go out to Iceland, to look to his promised maiden.

The earl said, " Now all ships bound for Iceland have sailed."

Then said one of the court: " Here lay, yesterday, Hallfred Troublous-Skald, out under Agdaness."

The earl answered, " That may be well; he sailed hence five nights ago."

Then Earl Eric had Gunnlaug rowed out to Hallfred, who greeted him with joy; and forthwith a fair wind bore them from land, and they were right merry.

This was late in the summer : but now Hallfred said to Gunnlaug : " Hast thou heard of how Raven, the son of Onund, is wooing Helga the Fair ? "

Gunnlaug said he had heard thereof, but dimly. Hallfred tells him all he knew of it, and therewith, too, that it was the talk of many men that Raven was in nowise less brave a man than Gunnlaug.

Then Gunnlaug sang this stave :—

> " Light the weather wafteth ;
> But if this east wind drifted
> Week-long, wild upon us
> Little were I recking ;
> More this word I mind of
> Me with Raven mated,
> Than gain for me the gold-foe
> Of days to make me grey-haired."

Then Hallfred said, "Well, fellow, may'st thou fare better in thy strife with Raven than I did in mine. I brought my ship some winters ago into Leiruvag, and had to pay a half-mark in silver to a house-carle of Raven's, but I held it back from him. So Raven rode at us with sixty men, and cut the moorings of the ship, and she was driven up on the shallows, and we were bound for a wreck. Then I had to give selfdoom to Raven, and a whole mark I had to pay ; and that is the tale of my dealings with him."

Then they two talked together alone of Helga the Fair, and Gunnlaug praised her much for her goodliness ; and Gunnlaug sang :—

> " He who brand of battle
> Beareth over-wary,
> Never love shall let him
> Hold the linen-folded ;
> For we when we were younger
> In many a way were playing
> On the outward nesses
> From golden land outstanding."

" Well sung ! " said Hallfred.

CHAPTER XII

OF GUNNLAUG'S LANDING, AND HOW HE
FOUND HELGA WEDDED TO RAVEN

THEY made land north by Fox-Plain in
Hraunhaven, half a month before winter,
and there unshipped their goods. Now there
was a man called Thord, a bonder's son of the
Plain, there. He fell to wrestling with the chapmen, and they mostly got worsted at his hands.

Then a wrestling was settled between him and
Gunnlaug. The night before Thord made vows
to Thor for the victory; but the next day, when
they met, they fell-to wrestling. Then Gunnlaug tripped both feet from under Thord, and
gave him a great fall; but the foot that Gunnlaug stood on was put out of joint, and Gunnlaug
fell together with Thord.

Then said Thord : "Maybe that other things
go no better for thee."

"What then?" says Gunnlaug.

"Thy dealings with Raven, if he wed Helga
the Fair at winter-nights. I was anigh at the
Thing when that was settled last summer."

Gunnlaug answered naught thereto.

Now the foot was swathed, and put into joint again, and it swelled mightily; but he and Hall-fred ride twelve in company till they come to Gilsbank, in Burg-firth, the very Saturday night when folk sat at the wedding at Burg. Illugi was fain of his son Gunnlaug and his fellows; but Gunnlaug said he would ride then and there down to Burg. Illugi said it was not wise to do so, and to all but Gunnlaug that seemed good. But Gunnlaug was then unfit to walk, because of his foot, though he would not let that be seen. Therefore there was no faring to Burg.

On the morrow Hallfred rode to Hreda-water, in North-water dale, where Galti, his brother and a brisk man, managed their matters.

CHAPTER XIII

OF THE WINTER-WEDDING AT SKANEY, AND HOW GUNNLAUG GAVE THE KING'S CLOAK TO HELGA

TELLS the tale of Raven, that he sat at his wedding-feast at Burg, and it was the talk of most men that the bride was but drooping; for true is the saw that saith, "Long we remember what youth gained us," and even so it was with her now.

But this new thing befell at the feast, that Hungerd, the daughter of Thorod and Jofrid, was wooed by a man named Sverting, the son of Hafr-Biorn, the son of Mold-Gnup, and the wedding was to come off that winter after Yule, at Skaney, where dwelt Thorkel, a kinsman of Hungerd, and son of Torfi Valbrandsson; and the mother of Torfi was Thorodda, the sister of Odd of the Tongue.

Now Raven went home to Mossfell with Helga his wife. When they had been there a little while, one morning early before they rose up, Helga was awake, but Raven slept, and fared ill in his sleep. And when he woke

Helga asked him what he had dreamt. Then Raven sang :—

> "In thine arms, so dreamed I,
> Hewn was I, gold island !
> Bride, in blood I bled there,
> Bed of thine was reddened.
> Never more then mightst thou,
> Mead-bowls' pourer speedy,
> Bind my gashes bloody—
> Lind-leek-bough thou lik'st it."

Helga spake : "Never shall I weep therefor," quoth she; "ye have evilly beguiled me, and Gunnlaug has surely come out." And therewith she wept much.

But, a little after, Gunnlaug's coming was bruited about, and Helga became so hard with Raven, that he could not keep her at home at Mossfell; so that back they had to go to Burg, and Raven got small share of her company.

Now men get ready for the winter-wedding. Thorkel of Skaney bade Illugi the Black and his sons. But when master Illugi got ready, Gunnlaug sat in the hall, and stirred not to go. Illugi went up to him and said, "Why dost thou not get ready, kinsman?"

Gunnlaug answered, "I have no mind to go."

Says Illugi, "Nay, but certes thou shalt go, kinsman," says he; "and cast thou not grief over thee by yearning for one woman. Make as if thou knewest nought of it, for women thou wilt never lack."

Now Gunnlaug did as his father bade him; so

they came to the wedding, and Illugi and his sons were set down in the high seat; but Thorstein Egilson, and Raven his son-in-law, and the bridegroom's following, were set in the other high seat, over against Illugi.

The women sat on the daïs, and Helga the Fair sat next to the bride. Oft she turned her eyes on Gunnlaug, thereby proving the saw, "Eyes will bewray if maid love man."

Gunnlaug was well arrayed, and had on him that goodly raiment that. King Sigtrygg had given him; and now he was thought far above all other men, because of many things, both strength, and goodliness, and growth.

There was little mirth among folk at this wedding. But on the day when all men were making ready to go away the women stood up and got ready to go home. Then went Gunnlaug to talk to Helga, and long they talked together: but Gunnlaug sang :—

> "Light-heart lived the Worm-tongue
> All day long no longer
> In mountain-home, since Helga
> Had name of wife of Raven;
> Nought foresaw thy father,
> Hardener white of fight-thaw,
> What my words should come to.
> —The maid to gold was wedded."

And again he sang :—

> "Worst reward I owe them,
> Father thine, O wine-may,
> And mother, that they made thee
> So fair beneath thy maid-gear;

D

For thou, sweet field of sea-flame,
All joy hast slain within me.—
Lo, here, take it, loveliest
E'er made of lord and lady!''

And therewith Gunnlaug gave Helga the cloak, Ethelred's gift, which was the fairest of things, and she thanked him well for the gift.

Then Gunnlaug went out, and by that time riding-horses had been brought home and saddled, and among them were many very good ones; and they were all tied up in the road. Gunnlaug leaps on to a horse, and rides a hand-gallop along the homefield up to a place where Raven happened to stand just before him; and Raven had to draw out of his way. Then Gunnlaug said—

"No need to slink aback, Raven, for I threaten thee nought as at this time; but thou knowest forsooth, what thou hast earned."

Raven answered and sang :—

" God of wound-flames glitter,
Glorier of fight-goddess,
Must we fall a-fighting
For fairest kirtle-bearer ?
Death-staff, many such-like
Fair as she is are there
In south-lands o'er the sea-floods.
Sooth saith he who knoweth."

" Maybe there are many such, but they do not seem so to me," said Gunnlaug.

Therewith Illugi and Thorstein ran up to them and would not have them fight.

Then Gunnlaug sang :—

> "The fair-hued golden goddess
> For gold to Raven sold they,
> (Raven my match as men say)
> While the mighty isle-king,
> Ethelred, in England
> From eastward way delayed me,
> Wherefore to gold-waster
> Waneth tongue's speech-hunger."

Hereafter both rode home, and all was quiet and tidingless that winter through ; but Raven had nought of Helga's fellowship after her meeting with Gunnlaug.

CHAPTER XIV

OF THE HOLMGANG AT THE ALTHING

NOW in summer men ride a very many to the Althing : Illugi the Black, and his sons with him, Gunnlaug and Hermund ; Thorstein Egilson and Kolsvein his son ; Onund, of Mossfell, and his sons all, and Sverting, Hafr-Biorn's son. Skapti yet held the spokesmanship-at-law.

One day at the Thing, as men went thronging to the Hill of Laws, and when the matters of the law were done there, then Gunnlaug craved silence, and said—

"Is Raven, the son of Onund, here?"

He said he was.

Then spake Gunnlaug, "Thou well knowest that thou hast got to wife my avowed bride, and thus hast thou made thyself my foe. Now for this I bid thee to holm here at the Thing, in the holm of the Axe-water, when three nights are gone by."

Raven answers, "This is well bidden, as was to be looked for of thee, and for this I am ready, whenever thou willest it."

Now the kin of each deemed this a very ill thing. But, at that time it was lawful for him who thought himself wronged by another to call him to fight on the holm.

So when three nights had gone by they got ready for the holmgang, and Illugi the Black followed his son thither with a great following. But Skapti, the lawman, followed Raven, and his father and other kinsmen of his.

Now before Gunnlaug went upon the holm he sang :—

> " Out to isle of eel-field
> Dight am I to hie me :
> Give, O God, thy singer
> With glaive to end the striving.
> Here shall I the head cleave
> Of Helga's love's devourer,
> At last my bright sword bringeth
> Sundering of head and body."

Then Raven answered and sang :—

> " Thou, singer, knowest not surely
> Which of us twain shall gain it ;
> With edge for leg-swathe eager,
> Here are the wound-scythes bare now.
> In whatso-wise we wound us,
> The tidings from the Thing here,
> And fame of thanes' fair doings,
> The fair young maid shall hear it."

Hermund held shield for his brother, Gunnlaug; but Sverting, Hafr-Biorn's son, was Raven's shield-bearer. Whoso should be wounded was to ransom himself from the holm with three marks of silver.

Now, Raven's part it was to deal the first blow, as he was the challenged man. He hewed at the

upper part of Gunnlaug's shield, and the sword
brake asunder just beneath the hilt, with so great
might he smote; but the point of the sword flew
up from the shield and struck Gunnlaug's cheek,
whereby he got just grazed; with that their fathers
ran in between them, and many other men.

"Now," said Gunnlaug, "I call Raven overcome, as he is weaponless."

"But I say that thou art vanquished, since thou
art wounded," said Raven.

Now, Gunnlaug was nigh mad, and very wrath-
ful, and said it was not tried out yet.

Illugi, his father, said they should try no more
for that time.

Gunnlaug said, "Beyond all things I desire that
I might in such wise meet Raven again, that thou,
father, wert not anigh to part us."

And thereat they parted for that time, and all
men went back to their booths.

But on the second day after this it was made law
in the law-court that, henceforth, all holmgangs
should be forbidden; and this was done by the
counsel of all the wisest men that were at the
Thing; and there, indeed, were all the men of
most counsel in all the land. And this was the
last holmgang fought in Iceland, this, wherein
Gunnlaug and Raven fought.

But this Thing was the third most thronged
Thing that has been held in Iceland; the first was
after Njal's burning, the second after the Heath-
slaughters.

Now, one morning, as the brothers Hermund

and Gunnlaug went to Axe-water to wash, on the other side went many women towards the river, and in that company was Helga the Fair.   Then said Hermund—

"Dost thou see thy friend Helga there on the other side of the river?"

"Surely, I see her," says Gunnlaug, and withal he sang :—

> " Born was she for men's bickering :
> Sore bale hath wrought the war-stem,
> And I yearned ever madly
> To hold that oak-tree golden.
> To me then, me destroyer
> Of swan-mead's flame, unneedful
> This looking on the dark-eyed,
> This golden land's beholding."

Therewith they crossed the river, and Helga and Gunnlaug spake awhile together, and as the brothers crossed the river eastward back again, Helga stood and gazed long after Gunnlaug.

Then Gunnlaug looked back and sang :—

> " Moon of linen-lapped one,
> Leek-sea-bearing goddess,
> Hawk-keen out of heaven
> Shone all bright upon me ;
> But that eyelid's moonbeam
> Of gold-necklaced goddess
> Her hath all undoing
> Wrought, and me made nought of."

CHAPTER XV

HOW GUNNLAUG AND RAVEN AGREED TO GO EAST TO NORWAY, TO TRY THE MATTER AGAIN

NOW after these things were gone by men rode home from the Thing, and Gunnlaug dwelt at home at Gilsbank.

On a morning when he awoke all men had risen up, but he alone still lay abed; he lay in a shut-bed behind the seats. Now into the hall came twelve men, all full armed, and who should be there but Raven, Onund's son; Gunnlaug sprang up forthwith, and got to his weapons.

But Raven spake, "Thou art in risk of no hurt this time," quoth he, "but my errand hither is what thou shalt now hear: Thou didst call me to a holmgang last summer at the Althing, and thou didst not deem matters to be fairly tried therein; now I will offer thee this, that we both fare away from Iceland, and go abroad next summer, and go on holm in Norway, for there our kinsmen are not like to stand in our way."

Gunnlaug answered, "Hail to thy words, stoutest of men! this thine offer I take gladly;

and here, Raven, mayest thou have cheer as good as thou mayest desire."

"It is well offered," said Raven, "but this time we shall first have to ride away." Thereon they parted.

Now the kinsmen of both sore misliked them of this, but could in no wise undo it, because of the wrath of Gunnlaug and Raven; and, after all, that must betide that drew towards.

Now it is to be said of Raven that he fitted out his ship in Leiruvag; two men are named that went with him, sisters' sons of his father Onund, one hight Grim, the other Olaf, doughty men both. All the kinsmen of Raven thought it great scathe when he went away, but he said he had challenged Gunnlaug to the holmgang because he could have no joy soever of Helga; and he said, withal, that one must fall before the other.

So Raven put to sea, when he had wind at will, and brought his ship to Thrandheim, and was there that winter and heard nought of Gunnlaug that winter through; there he abode him the summer following: and still another winter was he in Thrandheim, at a place called Lifangr.

Gunnlaug Worm-tongue took ship with Hall-fred Troublous-Skald, in the north at The Plain; they were very late ready for sea.

They sailed into the main when they had a fair wind, and made Orkney a little before the winter. Earl Sigurd Lodverson was still lord over the isles, and Gunnlaug went to him and abode there that winter, and the earl held him of much account.

In the spring the earl would go on warfare, and Gunnlaug made ready to go with him ; and that summer they harried wide about the South-isles and Scotland's firths, and had many fights, and Gunnlaug always showed himself the bravest and doughtiest of fellows, and the hardiest of men wherever they came.

Earl Sigurd went back home early in the summer, but Gunnlaug took ship with chapmen, sailing for Norway, and he and Earl Sigurd parted in great friendship.

Gunnlaug fared north to Thrandheim, to Hladir, to see Earl Eric, and dwelt there through the early winter ; the earl welcomed him gladly, and made offer to Gunnlaug to stay with him, and Gunnlaug agreed thereto.

The earl had heard already how all had be-fallen between Gunnlaug and Raven, and he told Gunnlaug that he laid ban on their fighting within his realm ; Gunnlaug said the earl should be free to have his will herein.

So Gunnlaug abode there the winter through, ever heavy of mood.

CHAPTER XVI

HOW THE TWO FOES MET AND FOUGHT
AT DINGNESS

BUT on a day in spring Gunnlaug was walking abroad, and his kinsman Thorkel with him; they walked away from the town, till on the meads before them they saw a ring of men, and in that ring were two men with weapons fencing; but one was named Raven, the other Gunnlaug, while they who stood by said that Icelanders smote light, and were slow to remember their words.

Gunnlaug saw the great mocking hereunder, and much jeering was brought into the play; and withal he went away silent.

So a little while after he said to the earl that he had no mind to bear any longer the jeers and mocks of his courtiers about his dealings with Raven, and therewith he prayed the earl to give him a guide to Lifangr: now before this the earl had been told that Raven had left Lifangr and gone east to Sweden; therefore, he granted Gunnlaug leave to go, and gave him two guides for the journey.

Now Gunnlaug went from Hladir with six

men to Lifangr; and, on the morning of the
very day whereas Gunnlaug came in in the
evening, Raven had left Lifangr with four men.
Thence Gunnlaug went to Vera-dale, and came
always in the evening to where Raven had been
the night before.

So Gunnlaug went on till he came to the
uppermost farm in the valley, called Sula, where-
from had Raven fared in the morning; there he
stayed not his journey, but kept on his way
through the night.

Then in the morning at sun-rise they saw one
another. Raven had got to a place where were
two waters, and between them flat meads, and
they are called Gleipni's meads: but into one
water stretched a little ness called Dingness.
There on the ness Raven and his fellows, five
together, took their stand. With Raven were
his kinsmen, Grim and Olaf.

Now when they met, Gunnlaug said, "It is
well that we have found one another."

Raven said that he had nought to quarrel
with therein; "But now," says he, "thou mayest
choose as thou wilt, either that we fight alone
together, or that we fight all of us man to man."

Gunnlaug said that either way seemed good
to him.

Then spake Raven's kinsmen, Grim and Olaf,
and said that they would little like to stand by
and look on the fight, and in like wise spake
Thorkel the Black, the kinsman of Gunnlaug.

Then said Gunnlaug to the earl's guides, "Ye

shall sit by and aid neither side, and be here to
tell of our meeting;" and so they did.

So they set on, and fought dauntlessly, all
of them.   Grim and Olaf went both against
Gunnlaug alone, and so closed their dealings
with him that Gunnlaug slew them both and
got no wound.   This proves Thord Kolbeinson
in a song that he made on Gunnlaug the Worm-
tongue :—

> " Grim and Olaf, great-hearts
> In Gondul's din, with thin sword
> First did Gunnlaug fell there
> Ere at Raven fared he ;
> Bold, with blood be-drifted
> Bane of three the thane was ;
> War-lord of the wave-horse
> Wrought for men folks' slaughter."

Meanwhile Raven and Thorkel the Black,
Gunnlaug's kinsman, fought until Thorkel fell
before Raven and lost his life ; and so at last
all their fellowship fell.   Then they two alone
fought together with fierce onsets and mighty
strokes, which they dealt each the other, falling
on furiously without stop or stay.

Gunnlaug had the sword Ethelred's-gift, and
that was the best of weapons.   At last Gunnlaug
dealt a mighty blow at Raven, and cut his leg
from under him ; but none the more did Raven
fall, but swung round up to a tree-stem, whereat
he steadied the stump.

Then said Gunnlaug, "Now thou art no more
meet for battle, nor will I fight with thee any
longer, a maimed man."

Raven answered: "So it is," said he, "that my lot is now all the worser lot, but it were well with me yet, might I but drink somewhat."

Gunnlaug said, "Bewray me not if I bring thee water in my helm."

"I will not bewray thee," said Raven.

Then went Gunnlaug to a brook and fetched water in his helm, and brought it to Raven; but Raven stretched forth his left hand to take it, but with his right hand drave his sword into Gunnlaug's head, and that was a mighty great wound.

Then Gunnlaug said, "Evilly hast thou beguiled me, and done traitorously wherein I trusted thee."

Raven answers, "Thou sayest sooth, but this brought me to it, that I begrudged thee to lie in the bosom of Helga the Fair."

Thereat they fought on, recking of nought; but the end of it was that Gunnlaug overcame Raven, and there Raven lost his life.

Then the earl's guides came forward and bound the head-wound of Gunnlaug, and in meanwhile he sat and sang :—

> "O thou sword-storm stirrer,
> Raven, stem of battle
> Famous, fared against me
> Fiercely in the spear din.
> Many a flight of metal
> Was borne on me this morning,
> By the spear-walls' builder,
> Ring-bearer, on hard Dingness."

After that they buried the dead, and got
Gunnlaug on to his horse thereafter, and brought
him right down to Lifangr.   There he lay three
nights, and got all his rights of a priest, and
died thereafter, and was buried at the church
there.

All men thought it great scathe of both of
these men, Gunnlaug and Raven, amid such
deeds as they died.

CHAPTER XVII

THE NEWS OF THE FIGHT BROUGHT TO ICELAND

NOW this summer, before these tidings were brought out hither to Iceland, Illugi the Black, being at home at Gilsbank, dreamed a dream: he thought that Gunnlaug came to him in his sleep, all bloody, and he sang in the dream this stave before him; and Illugi remembered the song when he woke, and sang it before others:—

> " Knew I of the hewing
> Of Raven's hilt-finned steel-fish
> Byrny-shearing—sword-edge
> Sharp clave leg of Raven.—
> Of warm wounds drank the eagle,
> When the war-rod slender,
> Cleaver of the corpses,
> Clave the head of Gunnlaug."

This portent befel south at Mossfell, the self-same night, that Onund dreamed how Raven came to him, covered all over with blood, and sang :—

> " Red is the sword, but I now
> Am undone by Sword-Odin.
> 'Gainst shields beyond the sea-flood
> The ruin of shields was wielded.

Methinks the blood-fowl blood-stained
In blood o'er men's heads stood there,
The wound-erne yet wound-eager
Trod over wounded bodies."

Now the second summer after this, Illugi the
Black spoke at the Althing from the Hill of
Laws, and said—

"Wherewith wilt thou make atonement to me
for my son, whom Raven, thy son, beguiled in
his troth?"

Onund answers, "Be it far from me to atone
for him, so sorely as their meeting hath wounded
me. Yet will I not ask atonement of thee for
my son."

"Then shall my wrath come home to some of
thy kin," says Illugi. And withal after the Thing
was Illugi at most times very sad.

Tells the tale how this autumn Illugi rode from
Gilsbank with thirty men, and came to Mossfell
early in the morning. Then Onund got into the
church with his sons, and took sanctuary; but
Illugi caught two of his kin, one called Biorn
and the other Thorgrim, and had Biorn slain,
but the feet smitten from Thorgrim. And thereafter Illugi rode home, and there was no righting
of this for Onund.

Hermund, Illugi's son, had little joy after the
death of Gunnlaug his brother, and deemed he
was none the more avenged even though this had
been wrought.

Now there was a man called Raven, brother's
son to Onund of Mossfell; he was a great sea-

E

farer, and had a ship that lay up in Ramfirth: and in the spring Hermund Illugison rode from home alone north over Holt-beacon Heath, even to Ramfirth, and out as far as Board-ere to the ship of the chapmen. The chapmen were then nearly ready for sea; Raven, the ship-master, was on shore, and many men with him; Hermund rode up to him, and thrust him through with his spear, and rode away forthwith: but all Raven's men were bewildered at seeing Hermund.

No atonement came for this slaying, and therewith ended the dealings of Illugi the Black and Onund of Mossfell.

CHAPTER XVIII

THE DEATH OF HELGA THE FAIR

AS time went on, Thorstein Egilson married his daughter Helga to a man called Thorkel, son of Hallkel, who lived west in Hraundale. Helga went to his house with him, but loved him little, for she cannot cease to think of Gunnlaug, though he be dead. Yet was Thorkel a doughty man, and wealthy of goods, and a good skald.

They had children together not a few, one of them was called Thorarin, another Thorstein, and yet more they had.

But Helga's chief joy was to pluck at the threads of that cloak, Gunnlaug's-gift, and she would be ever gazing at it.

But on a time there came a great sickness to the house of Thorkel and Helga, and many were bed-ridden for a long time. Helga also fell sick, and yet she could not keep abed.

So one Saturday evening Helga sat in the fire-hall, and leaned her head upon her husband's knees, and had the cloak Gunnlaug's-gift sent for; and when the cloak came to her she sat up and plucked at it, and gazed thereon awhile, and then sank back upon her husband's bosom, and was dead.   Then Thorkel sang this :—

"Dead in mine arms she droopeth,
My dear one, gold-rings bearer,
For God hath changed the life-days
Of this Lady of the linen.
Weary pain hath pined her,
But unto me, the seeker
Of hoard of fishes highway,
Abiding here is wearier."

Helga was buried in the church there, but Thorkel dwelt yet at Hraundale : but a great matter seemed the death of Helga to all, as was to be looked for.

AND HERE ENDETH THE STORY

THE STORY OF
FRITHIOF THE BOLD

THE STORY OF

FRITHIOF THE BOLD

CHAPTER I

OF KING BELI AND THORSTEIN VIKINGSON AND THEIR CHILDREN

THUS beginneth the tale, telling how that King Beli ruled over Sogn-land; three children had he, whereof Helgi was his first son, and Halfdan his second, but Ingibiorg his daughter. Ingibiorg was fair of face and wise of mind, and she was ever accounted the foremost of the king's children.

Now a certain strand went west of the firth, and a great stead was thereon, which was called Baldur's Meads; a Place of Peace was there, and a great temple, and round about it a great garth of pales: many gods were there, but amidst them all was Baldur held of most account. So jealous were the heathen men of this stead, that they would have no hurt done therein to man nor beast, nor might any man have dealings with a woman there.

Sowstrand was the name of that stead whereas

the king dwelt; but on the other side the firth
was an abode named Foreness, where dwelt a man
called Thorstein, the son of Viking; and his
stead was over against the king's dwelling.

Thorstein had a son by his wife called Frithiof:
he was the tallest and strongest of men, and more
furnished of all prowess than any other man,
even from his youth up. Frithiof the Bold was
he called, and so well beloved was he, that all
prayed for good things for him.

Now the king's children were but young when
their mother died; but a good man of Sogn,
named Hilding, prayed to have the king's
daughter to foster: so there was she reared well
and heedfully: and she was called Ingibiorg the
Fair. Frithiof also was fostered of goodman
Hilding, wherefore was he foster-brother to the
king's daughter, and they two were peerless
among children.

Now King Beli's chattels began to ebb fast
away from his hands, for he was grown old.

Thorstein had ruled over the third part of the
realm, and in him lay the king's greatest strength.

Every third year Thorstein feasted the king at
exceeding great cost, and the king feasted Thorstein the two years between.

Helgi, Beli's son, from his youth up turned
much to blood-offering: neither were those
brethren well-beloved.

Thorstein had a ship called Ellidi, which
pulled fifteen oars on either board; it ran up
high stem and stern, and was strong built like an

ocean-going ship, and its bulwarks were clamped with iron.

So strong was Frithiof that he pulled the two bow oars of Ellidi; but either oar was thirteen ells long, and two men pulled every oar otherwhere.

Frithiof was deemed peerless amid the young men of that time, and the king's sons envied him, whereas he was more praised than they.

Now King Beli fell sick; and when the sickness lay heavy on him he called his sons to him and said to them: "This sickness will bring me to mine end, therefore will I bid you this, that ye hold fast to those old friends that I have had; for meseems in all things ye fall short of that father and son, Thorstein and Frithiof, yea, both in good counsel and in hardihood. A mound ye shall raise over me."

So with that Beli died.

Thereafter Thorstein fell sick; so he spake to Frithiof: "Kinsman," says he, "I will crave this of thee, that thou bow thy will before the king's sons, for their dignity's sake; yet doth my heart speak goodly things to me concerning thy fortune. Now would I be laid in my mound over against King Beli's mound, down by the sea on this side the firth, whereas it may be easiest for us to cry out each to each of tidings drawing nigh."

A little after this Thorstein departed, and was laid in mound even as he had bidden; but Frithiof took the land and chattels after him. Biorn and Asmund were Frithiof's foster-brethren; they were big and strong men both.

CHAPTER II

FRITHIOF WOOETH INGIBIORG OF THOSE BRETHREN

SO Frithiof became the most famed of men, and the bravest in all things that may try a man.

Biorn, his foster-brother, he held in most account of all, but Asmund served the twain of them.

The ship Ellidi, he gat, the best of good things, of his father's heritage, and another possession therewith—a gold ring; no dearer was in Norway.

So bounteous a man was Frithiof withal, that it was the talk of most, that he was a man of no less honour than those brethren, but it were for the name of king; and for this cause they held Frithiof in hate and enmity, and it was a heavy thing to them that he was called greater than they: furthermore they thought they could see that Ingibiorg, their sister, and Frithiof were of one mind together.

It befell hereon that the kings had to go to a feast to Frithiof's house at Foreness; and there it happened according to wont that he gave to all men beyond that they were worthy of. Now Ingibiorg was there, and she and Frithiof talked

long together; and the king's daughter said to
him—

"A goodly gold ring hast thou."

"Yea, in good sooth," said he.

Thereafter went those brethren to their own
home, and greater grew their enmity of Frithiof.

A little after grew Frithiof heavy of mood,
and Biorn, his foster-brother, asked him why he
fared so.

He said he had it in his mind to woo Ingibiorg. "For though I be named by a lesser
name than those brethren, yet am I not fashioned
lesser."

"Even so let us do then," quoth Biorn. So
Frithiof fared with certain men unto those
brethren; and the kings were sitting on their
father's mound when Frithiof greeted them well,
and then set forth his wooing, and prayed for
their sister Ingibiorg, the daughter of Beli.

The kings said: "Not overwise is this thine
asking, whereas thou wouldst have us give her
to one who lacketh dignity; wherefore we gainsay
thee this utterly."

Said Frithiof: "Then is mine errand soon
sped; but in return never will I give help to you
henceforward, nay, though ye need it never so
much."

They said they heeded it nought: so Frithiof
went home, and was joyous once more.

CHAPTER III

OF KING RING AND THOSE BRETHREN

THERE was a king named Ring, who ruled over Ringrealm, which also was in Norway: a mighty folk-king he was, and a great man, but come by now unto his latter days.

Now he spake to his men : " Lo, I have heard that the sons of King Beli have brought to nought their friendship with Frithiof, who is the noblest of men ; wherefore will I send men to these kings, and bid them choose whether they will submit them to me and pay me tribute, or else that I bring war on them : and all things then shall lie ready to my hand to take, for they have neither might nor wisdom to withstand me ; yet great fame were it to my old age to overcome them."

After that fared the messengers of King Ring, and found those brethren, Helgi and Halfdan, in Sogn, and spake to them thus : "King Ring sends bidding to you to send him tribute, or else will he war against your realm."

They answered and said that they would not learn in the days of their youth what they would be loth to know in their old age, even how to

serve King Ring with shame. "Nay, now shall
we draw together all the folk that we may."

Even so they did; but now, when they beheld
their force that it was but little, they sent Hilding
their fosterer to Frithiof to bid him come help
them against King Ring. Now Frithiof sat at
the knave-play when Hilding came thither, who
spake thus: "Our kings send thee greeting,
Frithiof, and would have thy help in battle
against King Ring, who cometh against their
realm with violence and wrong."

Frithiof answered him nought, but said to
Biorn, with whom he was playing: "A bare
place in thy board, foster-brother, and nowise
mayst thou amend it; nay, for my part I shall
beset thy red piece there, and wot whether it be
safe."

Then Hilding spake again—

"King Helgi bade me say thus much, Frithiof,
that thou shouldst go on this journey with them,
or else look for ill at their hands when they at
the last come back."

"A double game, foster-brother," said Biorn;
"and two ways to meet thy play."

Frithiof said: "Thy play is to fall first on the
knave, yet the double game is sure to be."

No other outcome of his errand had Hilding:
he went back speedily to the kings, and told them
Frithiof's answer.

They asked Hilding what he made out of those
words. He said—

"Whereas he spake of the bare place he will

have been thinking of the lack in this journey
of yours; but when he said he would beset the
red piece, that will mean Ingibiorg, your sister;
so give ye all the heed ye may to her.   But
whereas I threatened him with ill from you, Biorn
deemed the game a double one ; but Frithiof said
that the knave must be set on first, speaking
thereby of King Ring."

So then the brethren arrayed them for departing ; but, ere they went, they let bring Ingibiorg
and eight women with her to Baldur's Meads,
saying that Frithiof would not be so mad rash
as to go see her thither, since there was none who
durst make riot there.

Then fared those brethren south to Jadar, and
met King Ring in Sokn-Sound.

Now, herewith was King Ring most of all
wroth that the brothers had said that they accounted it a shame to fight with a man so old
that he might not get a-horseback unholpen.

CHAPTER IV

FRITHIOF GOES TO BALDUR'S MEADS

STRAIGHTWAY whenas the kings were gone away Frithiof took his raiment of state and set the goodly gold ring on his arm; then went the foster-brethren down to the sea and launched Ellidi. Then said Biorn: "Whither away, foster-brother?"

"To Baldur's Meads," said Frithiof, "to be glad with Ingibiorg."

Biorn said: "A thing unmeet to do, to make the gods wroth with us."

"Well, it shall be risked this time," said Frithiof; "and withal, more to me is Ingibiorg's grace than Baldur's grame."

Therewith they rowed over the firth, and went up to Baldur's Meads and to Ingibiorg's bower, and there she sat with eight maidens, and the new comers were eight also.

But when they came there, lo, all the place was hung with cloth of pall and precious webs.

Then Ingibiorg arose and said:

"Why art thou so overbold, Frithiof, that thou art come here without the leave of my brethren to make the gods angry with thee?"

Frithiof says : " Howsoever that may be, I hold thy love of more account than the gods' hate."

Ingibiorg answered : "Welcome art thou here, thou and thy men ! "

Then she made place for him to sit beside her, and drank to him in the best of wine ; and thus they sat and were merry together.

Then beheld Ingibiorg the goodly ring on his arm, and asked him if that precious thing were his own.   Frithiof said Yea, and she praised the ring much.   Then Frithiof said :

" I will give thee the ring if thou wilt promise to give it to no one, but to send it to me when thou no longer shalt have will to keep it : and hereon shall we plight troth each to other."

So with this troth-plighting they exchanged rings.

Frithiof was oft at Baldur's Meads a-night time, and every day between whiles would he go thither to be glad with Ingibiorg.

CHAPTER V

THOSE BRETHREN COME HOME AGAIN

NOW tells the tale of those brethren, that they met King Ring, and he had more folk than they: then went men betwixt them, and sought to make peace, so that no battle should be : thereto King Ring assented on such terms that the brethren should submit them to him, and give him in marriage Ingibiorg their sister, with the third part of all their possessions.

The kings said Yea thereto, for they saw that they had to do with overwhelming might : so the peace was fast bound by oaths, and the wedding was to be at Sogn whenas King Ring should go see his betrothed.

So those brethren fare home with their folk, right ill content with things. But Frithiof, when he deemed that the brethren might be looked for home again, spake to the king's daughter—

"Sweetly and well have ye done to us, neither has goodman Baldur been wroth with us ; but now as soon as ye wot of the kings' coming home, spread the sheets of your beds abroad on the Hall of the Goddesses, for that is the highest of all the garth, and we may see it from our stead."

F

The king's daughter said: "Thou dost not after the like of any other : but certes, we welcome dear friends whenas ye come to us."

So Frithiof went home ; and the next morning he went out early, and when he came in then he spake and sang :—

> "Now must I tell
> To our good men
> That over and done
> Are our fair journeys ;
> No more a-shipboard
> Shall we be going,
> For there are the sheets
> Spread out a-bleaching."

Then they went out, and saw that the Hall of the Goddesses was all thatched with white linen. Biorn spake and said : "Now are the kings come home, and but a little while have we to sit in peace, and good were it, meseems, to gather folk together."

So did they, and men came flocking thither.

Now the brethren soon heard of the ways of Frithiof and Ingibiorg, and of the gathering of men. So King Helgi spake—

"A wondrous thing how Baldur will bear what shame soever Frithiof and she will lay on him! Now will I send men to him, and wot what atonement he will offer us, or else will I drive him from the land, for our strength seemeth to me not enough that we should fight with him as now."

So Hilding, their fosterer, bare the king's errand

to Frithiof and his friends, and spake in such wise: "This atonement the kings will have of thee, Frithiof, that thou go gather the tribute of the Orkneys, which has not been paid since Beli died, for they need money, whereas they are giving Ingibiorg their sister in marriage, and much of wealth with her."

Frithiof said: "This thing only somewhat urges us to peace, the good will of our kin departed; but no trustiness will those brethren show herein. But this condition I make, that our lands be in good peace while we are away." So this was promised and all bound by oaths.

Then Frithiof arrays him for departing, and is captain of men brave and of good help, eighteen in company.

Now his men asked him if he would not go to King Helgi and make peace with him, and pray himself free from Baldur's wrath.

But he answered: "Hereby I swear that I will never pray Helgi for peace."

Then he went aboard Ellidi, and they sailed out along the Sognfirth.

But when Frithiof was gone from home, King Halfdan spake to Helgi his brother: "Better lordship and more had we if Frithiof had payment for his masterful deed: now therefore let us burn his stead, and bring on him and his men such a storm on the sea as shall make an end of them."

Helgi said it was a thing meet to be done.

So then they burned up clean all the stead at

Foreness and robbed it of all goods; and after that sent for two witch-wives, Heidi and Hamglom, and gave them money to raise against Frithiof and his men so mighty a storm that they should all be lost at sea.   So they sped the witch-song, and went up on the witch-mount with spells and sorcery.

CHAPTER VI

FRITHIOF SAILS FOR THE ORKNEYS

SO when Frithiof and his men were come out of the Sognfirth there fell on them great wind and storm, and an exceeding heavy sea ; but the ship drave on swiftly, for sharp built she was, and the best to breast the sea.

So now Frithiof sang :—

> " Oft let I swim from Sogn
> My tarred ship sooty-sided,
> When maids sat o'er the mead-horn
> Amidst of Baldur's Meadows ;
> Now while the storm is wailing
> Farewell I bid you maidens,
> Still shall ye love us, sweet ones,
> Though Ellidi the sea fill."

Said Biorn : " Thou mightest find other work to do than singing songs over the maids of Baldur's Meadows."

" Of such work shall I not speedily run dry, though," said Frithiof. Then they bore up north to the sounds nigh those isles that are called Solundir, and therewith was the gale at its hardest.

Then sang Frithiof :—

> " Now is the sea a-swelling,
>   And sweepeth the rack onward ;
>   Spells of old days cast o'er us
>   Make ocean all unquiet ;
>   No more shall we be striving
>   Mid storm with wash of billows,
>   But Solundir shall shelter
>   Our ship with ice-beat rock-walls."

So they lay to under the lee of the isles hight
Solundir, and were minded to abide there ; but
straightway thereon the wind fell : then they
turned away from under the lee of the islands,
and now their voyage seemed hopeful to them,
because the wind was fair awhile : but soon it
began to freshen again.

Then sang Frithiof :—

> " In days foredone
>   From Foreness strand
>   I rowed to meet
>   Maid Ingibiorg ;
>   But now I sail
>   Through chilly storm
>   And wide away
>   My long-worm driveth."

And now when they were come far out into
the main, once more the sea waxed wondrous
troubled, and a storm arose with so great drift
of snow, that none might see the stem from the
stern : and they shipped seas, so that they must
be ever a-baling.   So Frithiof sang :—

> " The salt waves see we nought
>   As seaward drive we ever
>   Before the witch-wrought weather,
>   We well-famed kings'-defenders :

Here are we all a-standing,
With all Solundir hull-down,   -
Eighteen brave lads a-baling
Black Ellidi to bring home."

Said Biorn: "Needs must he who fareth far
fall in with diverse hap." "Yea, certes, foster-
brother," said Frithiof.   And he sang withal :—

"Helgi it is that helpeth
The white-head billows' waxing;
Cold time unlike the kissing
In the close of Baldur's Meadow !
So is the hate of Helgi
To that heart's love she giveth.
O would that here I held her,
Gift high above all giving ! ' "

"Maybe," said Biorn, "she is looking higher
than thou now art : what matter when all is
said ?"

"Well," says Frithiof, "now is the time to
show ourselves to be men of avail, though blither
tide it was at Baldur's Meadows."

So they turned to in manly wise, for there were
the bravest of men come together in the best ship
of the Northlands.   But Frithiof sang a stave :—

"So come in the West-sea,
Nought see I the billows,
The sea-water seemeth
As sweeping of wild-fire.
Topple the rollers,
Toss the hills swan-white,
Ellidi wallows
O'er steep of the wave-hills."

Then they shipped a huge sea, so that all stood a-baling. But Frithiof sang :—

> "With love-moved mouth the maiden
> Me pledgeth though I founder.
> Ah! bright sheets lay a-bleaching,
> East there on brents the swan loves."

Biorn said : "Art thou of mind belike that the maids of Sogn will weep many tears over thee ? "

Said Frithiof: "Surely that was in my mind."

Therewith so great a sea broke over the bows, that the water came in like the in-falling of a river ; but it availed them much that the ship was so good, and the crew aboard her so hardy.

Now sang Biorn :—

> "No widow, methinks,
> To thee or me drinks :
> No ring-bearer fair
> Biddeth draw near ;
> Salt are our eyne
> Soaked in the brine ;
> Strong our arms are no more,
> And our eyelids smart sore."

Quoth Asmund : "Small harm though your arms be tried somewhat, for no pity we had from you when we rubbed our eyes whenas ye must needs rise early a-mornings to go to Baldur's Meadows."

" Well," said Frithiof, " why singest thou not, Asmund ? "

" Not I," said Asmund ; yet sang a ditty straightway :—

" Sharp work about the sail was
When o'er the ship seas tumbled,
And there was I a-working
Within-board 'gainst eight balers ;
Better it was to bower,
Bringing the women breakfast,
Than here to be 'mid billows
Black Ellidi a-baling."

" Thou accountest thy help of no less worth than it is ? " said Frithiof, laughing therewith ; " but sure it showeth the thrall's blood in thee that thou wouldst fain be awaiting at table."

Now it blew harder and harder yet, so that to those who were aboard liker to huge peaks and mountains than to waves seemed the sea-breakers that crashed on all sides against the ship.

Then Frithiof sang :—

" On bolster I sat
In Baldur's Mead erst,
And all songs that I could
To the king's daughter sang ;
Now on Ran's bed belike
Must I soon be a-lying,
And another shall be
By Ingibiorg's side."

Biorn said : " Great fear lieth ahead of us, foster-brother, and now dread hath crept into thy words, which is ill with such a good man as thou."

Says Frithiof : " Neither fear nor fainting is it, though I sing now of those our merry journeys ; yet perchance more hath been said of them than need was : but most men would think death surer than life, if they were so bested as we be."

" Yet shall I answer thee somewhat," said Biorn, and sang :—

> " Yet one gain have I gotten
> Thou gatst not 'mid thy fortune,
> For meet play did I make me
> With Ingibiorg's eight maidens;
> Red rings we laid together
> Aright in Baldur's Meadow,
> When far off was the warder
> Of the wide land of Halfdan."

" Well," said he, " we must be content with things as they are, foster-brother."

Therewith so great a sea smote them, that the bulwark was broken and both the sheets, and four men were washed overboard and all lost.

Then sang Frithiof :—

> " Both sheets are bursten
> Amid the great billows,
> Four swains are sunk
> In the fathomless sea."

" Now, meseems," said Frithiof, " it may well be that some of us will go to the house of Ran, nor shall we deem us well sped if we come not thither in glorious array ; wherefore it seems good to me that each man of us here should have somewhat of gold on him."

Then he smote asunder the ring, Ingibiorg's gift, and shared it between all his men, and sang a stave withal :—

> " The red ring here I hew me
> Once owned of Halfdan's father,
> The wealthy lord of erewhile,
> Or the sea waves undo us,

> So on the guests shall gold be,
> If we have need of guesting;
> Meet so for mighty men-folk
> Amid Ran's hall to hold them."

"Not all so sure is it that we come there," said Biorn; "and yet it may well be so."

Now Frithiof and his folk found that the ship had great way on her, and they knew not what lay ahead, for all was mirk on either board, so that none might see the stem or stern from amidships; and therewith was there great drift of spray amid the furious wind, and frost, and snow, and deadly cold.

Now Frithiof went up to the masthead, and when he came down he said to his fellows: "A sight exceeding wondrous have I seen, for a great whale went in a ring about the ship, and I misdoubt me that we come nigh to some land, and that he is keeping the shore against us; for certes King Helgi has dealt with us in no friendly wise, neither will this his messenger be friendly. Moreover I saw two women on the back of the whale, and they it is who will have brought this great storm on us with the worst of spells and witchcraft; but now we shall try which may prevail, my fortune or their devilry, so steer ye at your straightest, and I will smite these evil things with beams."

Therewith he sang a stave :—

> "See I troll women
> Twain on the billows,
> E'en they whom Helgi
> Hither hath sent.

> Ellidi now
> Or ever her way stop
> Shall smite the backs
> Of these asunder."

So tells the tale that this wonder went with the good ship Ellidi, that she knew the speech of man.

But Biorn said : "Now may we see the treason of those brethren against us." Therewith he took the tiller, but Frithiof caught up a forked beam, and ran into the prow, and sang a stave :—

> "Ellidi, hail!
> Leap high o'er the billows!
> Break of the troll wives
> Brow or teeth now!
> Break cheek or jaw
> Of the cursed woman,
> One foot or twain
> Of the ogress filthy."

Therewith he drave his fork at one of the skin-changers, and the beak of Ellidi smote the other on the back, and the backs of both were broken ; but the whale took the deep, and gat him gone, and they never saw him after.

Then the wind fell, but the ship lay water-logged ; so Frithiof called out to his men, and bade bale out the ship, but Biorn said :—

"No need to work now, verily!"

"Be thou not afeard, foster-brother," said Frithiof, "ever was it the wont of good men of old time to be helpful while they might, whatsoever should come after."

And therewith he sang a stave :—

> "No need, fair fellows,
> To fear the death-day ;
> Rather be glad,
> Good men of mine :
> For if dreams wot aught
> All nights they say
> I yet shall have
> My Ingibiorg."

Then they baled out the ship; and they were now come nigh unto land ; but there was yet a flaw of wind in their teeth.   So then did Frithiof take the two bow oars again, and rowed full mightily. Therewith the weather brightened, and they saw that they were come out to Effia Sound, and so there they made land.

The crew were exceeding weary ; but so stout a man was Frithiof that he bore eight men a-land over the foreshore, but Biorn bore two, and Asmund one.   Then sang Frithiof :—

> " Fast bare I up
> To the fire-lit house
> My men all dazed
> With the drift of the storm :
> And the sail moreover
> To the sand I carried ;
> With the might of the sea
> Is there no more to do."

CHAPTER VII

FRITHIOF AT THE ORKNEYS

NOW Earl Angantyr was at Effia whenas
Frithiof and his folk came a-land there.
But his way it was, when he was sitting at the
drink, that one of his men should sit at the
watch-window, looking weatherward from the
drinking hall, and keep watch there. From a
great horn drank he ever: and still as one was
emptied another was filled for him. And he
who held the watch when Frithiof came a-land
was called Hallward; and now he saw where
Frithiof and his men went, and sang a stave :—

> " Men see I a-baling
>   Amid the storm's might ;
> Six bale on Ellidi
> Seven are a-rowing ;
> Like is he in the stem,
> Straining hard at the oars,
> To Frithiof the Bold,
> The brisk in the battle."

So when he had drunk out the horn, he cast it
in through the window, and spake to the woman
who gave him drink :—

"Take up from the floor,
O fair-going woman,
The horn cast adown
Drunk out to the end !
I behold men at sea
Who, storm-beaten, shall need
Help at our hands
Ere the haven they make."

Now the Earl heard what Hallward sang ; so he asked for tidings, and Hallward said : " Men are come a-land here, much forewearied, yet brave lads belike : but one of them is so hardy that he beareth the others ashore."

Then said the Earl, " Go ye, and meet them, and welcome them in seemly wise; if this be Frithiof, the son of Hersir Thorstein, my friend, he is a man famed far and wide for all prowess."

Then there took up the word a man named Atli, a great viking, and he spake : " Now shall that be proven which is told of, that Frithiof hath sworn never to be first in the craving of peace."

There were ten men in company with him, all evil and outrageous, who often wrought berserks-gang.

So when they met Frithiof they took to their weapons.

But Atli said—

" Good to turn hither, Frithiof ! Clutching ernes should claw ; and we no less, Frithiof ! Yea, and now may'st thou hold to thy word, and not crave first for peace."

So Frithiof turned to meet them, and sang a
stave :—

> " Nay, nay, in nought
> Now shall ye cow us.
> Blenching hearts
> Isle-abiders!
> Alone with you ten
> The fight will I try,
> Rather than pray
> For peace at your hands."

Then came Hallward thereto, and spake—
" The Earl wills that ye all be made welcome
here : neither shall any set on you."

Frithiof said he would take that with a good
heart; howsoever he was ready for either peace
or war.

So thereon they went to the Earl, and he made
Frithiof and all his men right welcome, and they
abode with him, in great honour holden, through
the wintertide; and oft would the Earl ask of
their voyage : so Biorn sang :—

> " There baled we, wight fellows,
> Washed over and over
> On both boards
> By billows;
> For ten days we baled there,
> And eight thereunto."

The Earl said : " Well nigh did the king undo
you ; it is ill seen of such-like kings as are meet
for nought but to overcome men by wizardry.
But now I wot," says Angantyr, "of thine errand
hither, Frithiof, that thou art sent after the scat :

whereto I give thee a speedy answer, that never shall King Helgi get scat of me, but to thee will I give money, even as much as thou wilt; and thou mayest call it scat if thou hast a mind to, or whatso else thou wilt."

So Frithiof said that he would take the money.

G

CHAPTER VIII

KING RING WEDDETH INGIBIORG

NOW shall it be told of what came to pass in Norway the while Frithiof was away: for those brethren let burn up all the stead at Foreness. Moreover, while the weird sisters were at their spells they tumbled down from off their high witch-mount, and brake both their backs.

That autumn came King Ring north to Sogn to his wedding, and there at a noble feast drank his bridal with Ingibiorg.

"Whence came that goodly ring which thou hast on thine arm?" said King Ring to Ingibiorg.

She said her father had owned it, but he answered and said—

"Nay, for Frithiof's gift it is: so take it off thine arm straightway; for no gold shalt thou lack whenas thou comest to Elfhome."

So she gave the ring to King Helgi's wife, and bade her give it to Frithiof when he came back.

Then King Ring wended home with his wife, and loved her with exceeding great love,

CHAPTER IX

FRITHIOF BRINGS THE TRIBUTE TO THE KINGS

THE spring after these things Frithiof departed from the Orkneys and Earl Angantyr in all good liking; and Hallward went with Frithiof.

But when they came to Norway they heard tell of the burning of Frithiof's stead.

So when he was gotten to Foreness, Frithiof said: "Black is my house waxen now; no friends have been at work here." And he sang withal :—

> "Frank and free,
> With my father dead,
> In Foreness old
> We drank aforetime.
> Now my abode
> Behold I burned;
> For many ill deeds
> The kings must I pay."

Then he sought rede of his men what was to be done; but they bade him look to it: then he said that the scat must first be paid out of hand. So they rowed over the Firth to Sowstrand; and

there they heard that the kings were gone to
Baldur's Meads to sacrifice to the gods; so
Frithiof and Biorn went up thither, and bade
Hallward and Asmund break up meanwhile all
ships, both great and small, that were anigh; and
they did so.   Then went Frithiof and his fellow
to the door at Baldur's Meads, and Frithiof would
go in.   Biorn bade him fare warily, since he must
needs go in alone; but Frithiof charged him to
abide without, and keep watch; and he sang a
stave :—

> " All alone go I
> Unto the stead;
> No folk I need
> For the finding of kings;
> But cast ye the fire
> O'er the kings' dwelling,
> If I come not again
> In the cool of the even."

"Ah," said Biorn, "a goodly singing!"

Then went Frithiof in, and saw but few folk in
the Hall of the Goddesses; there were the kings
at their blood-offering, sitting a-drinking; a fire
was there on the floor, and the wives of the
kings sat thereby, a-warming the gods, while
others anointed them, and wiped them with
napkins.

So Frithiof went up to King Helgi and said:
"Have here thy scat!"

And therewith he heaved up the purse wherein
was the silver, and drave it on to the face of the
king; whereby were two of his teeth knocked out,
and he fell down stunned in his high seat; but

Halfdan got hold of him, so that he fell not into the fire. Then sang Frithiof :—-

> " Have here thy scat,
> High lord of the warriors !
> Heed that and thy teeth,
> Lest all tumble about thee !
> Lo the silver abideth
> At the bight of this bag here,
> That Biorn and I
> Betwixt us have borne thee."

Now there were but few folk in the chamber, because the drinking was in another place; so Frithiof went out straightway along the floor, and beheld therewith that goodly ring of his on the arm of Helgi's wife as she warmed Baldur at the fire; so he took hold of the ring, but it was fast to her arm, and he dragged her by it over the pavement toward the door, and Baldur fell from her into the fire; then Halfdan's wife caught hastily at Baldur, whereby the god that she was warming fell likewise into the fire, and the fire caught both the gods, for they had been anointed, and ran up thence into the roof, so that the house was all ablaze : but Frithiof got the ring to him ere he came out.

So then Biorn asked him what had come of his going in there; but Frithiof held up the ring and sang a stave :—

> " The heavy purse smote Helgi
> Hard 'midst his scoundrel's visage :
> Lowly bowed Halfdan's brother,
> Fell bundling 'mid the high seat :

'There Baldur fell a-burning.
But first my bright ring gat I.
Fast from the roaring fire
I dragged the bent crone forward.''

Men say that Frithiof cast a firebrand up on
to the roof, so that the hall was all ablaze, and
therewith sang a stave :—

" Down stride we toward the sea-strand,
And strong deeds set a-going,
For now the blue flame bickers
Amidst of Baldur's Meadow."

And therewith they went down to the sea.

CHAPTER X

FRITHIOF MADE AN OUTLAW

BUT as soon as King Helgi had come to himself he bade follow after Frithiof speedily, and slay them all, him and his fellows : "A man of forfeit life, who spareth no Place of Peace!"

So they blew the gathering for the king's men, and when they came out to the hall they saw that it was afire; so King Halfdan went thereto with some of the folk, but King Helgi followed after Frithiof and his men, who were by then gotten a-shipboard and were lying on their oars.

Now King Helgi and his men find that all the ships are scuttled, and they have to turn back to shore, and have lost some men : then waxed King Helgi so wroth that he grew mad, and he bent his bow, and laid an arrow on the string, and drew at Frithiof so mightily that the bow brake asunder in the midst.

But when Frithiof saw that, then he gat him to the two bow oars of Ellidi, and laid so hard on them that they both brake, and with that he sang a stave :—

> "Young Ingibiorg
> Kissed I aforetime,
> Kissed Beli's daughter
> In Baldur's Meadow.

> So shall the oars
> Of Ellidi
> Break both together
> As Helgi's bow breaks."

Then the land-wind ran down the firth and they hoisted sail and sailed; but Frithiof bade them look to it that they might have no long abiding there. And so withal they sailed out of the Sognfirth, and Frithiof sang :—

> "Sail we away from Sogn,
> E'en as we sailed aforetime,
> When flared the fire all over
> The house that was my father's.
> Now is the bale a-burning
> Amidst of Baldur's Meadow :
> But wend I as a wild-wolf,
> Well wot I they have sworn it."

"What shall we turn to now, foster-brother?" said Biorn.

"I may not abide here in Norway," said Frithiof: "I will learn the ways of warriors, and sail a-warring."

So they searched the isles and out-skerries the summer long, and gathered thereby riches and renown; but in autumn-tide they made for the Orkneys, and Angantyr gave them good welcome, and they abode there through the winter-tide.

But when Frithiof was gone from Norway the kings held a Thing, whereat was Frithiof made an outlaw throughout their realm : they took his lands to them, moreover, and King Halfdan took up his abode at Foreness, and built up again all

Baldur's Meadow, though it was long ere the
fire was slaked there. This misliked King Helgi
most, that the gods were all burned up, and great
was the cost or ever Baldur's Meadow was built
anew fully equal to its first estate.

So King Helgi abode still at Sowstrand.

CHAPTER XI

FRITHIOF FARETH TO SEE KING RING
AND INGIBIORG

FRITHIOF waxed ever in riches and renown whithersoever he went: evil men he slew, and grimly strong-thieves, but husbandmen and chapmen he let abide in peace; and now was he called anew Frithiof the Bold; he had gotten to him by now a great company well arrayed, and was become exceeding wealthy of chattels.

But when Frithiof had been three winters a-warring he sailed west, and made the Wick; then he said that he would go a-land: "But ye shall fare a-warring without me this winter; for I begin to weary of warfare, and would fain go to the Uplands, and get speech of King Ring: but hither shall ye come to meet me in the summer, and I will be here the first day of summer."

Biorn said: "This counsel is naught wise, though thou must needs rule; rather would I that we fare north to Sogn, and slay both those kings, Helgi and Halfdan."

"It is all naught," said Frithiof; "I must needs go see King Ring and Ingibiorg."

Says Biorn: "Loth am I hereto that thou shouldst risk thyself alone in his hands; for this Ring is a wise man and of great kin, though he be somewhat old."

But Frithiof said he would have his own way: "And thou, Biorn, shalt be captain of our company meanwhile."

So they did as he bade, and Frithiof fared to the Uplands in the autumn, for he desired sore to look upon the love of King Ring and Ingibiorg. But or ever he came there he did on him, over his clothes, a great cloak all shaggy; two staves he had in his hand, and a mask over his face, and he made as if he were exceeding old.

So he met certain herdsmen, and, going heavily, he asked them: "Whence are ye?" They answered and said: "We are of Streitaland, whereas the king dwelleth."

Quoth the carle: "Is King Ring a mighty king, then?"

They answered: "Thou lookest to us old enough to have cunning to know what manner of man is King Ring in all wise."

The carle said that he had heeded salt-boiling more than the ways of kings; and therewith he goes up to the king's house.

So when the day was well worn he came into the hall, blinking about as a dotard, and took an outward place, pulling his hood over him to hide his visage.

Then spake King Ring to Ingibiorg: "There is come into the hall a man far bigger than other men."

The queen answered : "That is no such great tidings here."

But the king spake to a serving-man who stood before the board, and said : "Go thou, and ask yon cowled man who he is, whence he cometh, and of what kin he is."

So the lad ran down the hall to the new-comer and said : "What art thou called, thou man? Where wert thou last night? Of what kin art thou?"

Said the cowled man : "Quick come thy questions, good fellow! but hast thou skill to understand if I shall tell thee hereof?"

"Yea, certes," said the lad.

"Well," said the cowl-bearer, "Thief is my name, with Wolf was I last night, and in Grief-ham was I reared."

Then ran the lad back to the king, and told him the answer of the new-comer.

"Well told, lad," said the king; "but for that land of Grief-ham, I know it well: it may well be that the man is of no light heart, and yet a wise man shall he be, and of great worth I account him."

Said the queen: "A marvellous fashion of thine, that thou must needs talk so freely with every carle that cometh hither! Yea, what is the worth of him, then?"

'That wottest thou no clearer than I," said the king; "but I see that he thinketh more than he talketh, and is peering all about him."

Therewith the king sent a man after him, and

so the cowl-bearer went up before the king, going somewhat bent, and greeted him in a low voice. Then said the king: "What art thou called, thou big man?"

And the cowl-bearer answered and sang:—

> "PEACE-THIEF they called me
> On the prow with the Vikings;
> But WAR-THIEF whenas
> I set widows a-weeping;
> SPEAR-THIEF when I
> Sent forth the barbed shafts;
> BATTLE-THIEF when I
> Burst forth on the king;
> HEL-THIEF when I
> Tossed up the small babies:
> ISLE-THIEF when I
> In the outer isles harried;
> SLAINS-THIEF when I
> Sat aloft over men:
> Yet since have I drifted
> With salt-boiling carls,
> Needy of help
> Ere hither I came."

Said the king: "Thou hast gotten thy name of Thief from many a matter, then; but where wert thou last night, and what is thy home?"

The cowl-bearer said: "In Grief-ham I grew up; but heart drave me hither, and home have I nowhere."

The king said: "Maybe indeed that thou hast been nourished in Grief-ham a certain while; yet also maybe that thou wert born in a place of peace. But in the wild-wood must thou have lain last night, for no goodman dwelleth anigh named Wolf; but whereas thou sayest thou hast no home, so is it, that thou belike deemest thy home nought, because of thy heart that drave thee hither."

Then spake Ingibiorg: "Go, Thief, get thee to some other harbour, or in to the guest-hall."

"Nay," said the king, "I am old enow to know how to marshal guests; so do off thy cowl, new-comer, and sit down on my other hand."

"Yea, old, and over old," said the queen, "when thou settest staff-carles by thy side."

"Nay, lord, it beseemeth not," said Thief; "better it were as the queen sayeth. I have been more used to boiling salt than sitting beside lords."

"Do thou my will," said the king, "for I will rule this time."

So Thief cast his cowl from him, and was clad thereunder in a dark blue kirtle; on his arm, moreover, was the goodly gold ring, and a thick silver belt was round about him, with a great purse on it, and therein silver pennies glittering; a sword was girt to his side, and he had a great fur hood on his head, for his eyes were bleared, and his face all wrinkled.

"Ah! now we fare better, say I," quoth the king; "but do thou, queen, give him a goodly mantle, well shapen for him."

"Thou shalt rule, my lord," said the queen; "but in small account do I hold this Thief of thine."

So then he gat a good mantle over him, and sat down in the high-seat beside the king.

The queen waxed red as blood when she saw the goodly ring, yet would she give him never a word; but the king was exceeding blithe with him and said: "A goodly ring hast thou on thine arm there; thou must have boiled salt long enough to get it."

Says he, "That is all the heritage of my father."

"Ah!" says the king, "maybe thou hast more than that; well, few salt-boiling carles are thy peers, I deem, unless eld is deep in mine eyes now."

So Thief was there through the winter amid good entertainment, and well accounted of by all men; he was bounteous of his wealth, and joyous with all men: the queen held but little converse with him; but the king and he were ever blithe together.

CHAPTER XII

FRITHIOF SAVES THE KING AND QUEEN ON THE ICE

THE tale tells that on a time King Ring and the queen, and a great company, would go to a feast. So the king spake to Thief: "Wilt thou fare with us, or abide at home?"

He said he had liefer go; and the king said: "Then am I the more content."

So they went on their ways, and had to cross a certain frozen water. Then said Thief: "I deem this ice untrustworthy; meseemeth ye fare unwarily."

Quoth the king: "It is often shown how heedful in thine heart thou wilt be to us."

So a little after the ice broke in beneath them, and Thief ran thereto, and dragged the wain to him, with all that was therein; and the king and the queen both sat in the same: so Thief drew it all up on to the ice, with the horses that were yoked to the wain.

Then spake King Ring: "Right well drawn, Thief! Frithiof the Bold himself would have drawn no stronger had he been here; doughty followers are such as thou!"

So they came to the feast, and there is nought to tell thereof, and the king went back again with seemly gifts.

CHAPTER XIII

THE KING SLEEPS BEFORE FRITHIOF

NOW weareth away the mid-winter, and when spring cometh, the weather groweth fair, the wood bloometh, the grass groweth, and ships may glide betwixt land and land. So on a day the king says to his folk: "I will that ye come with us for our disport out into the woods, that we may look upon the fairness of the earth."

So did they, and went flock-meal with the king into the woods; but so it befell, that the king and Frithiof were gotten alone together afar from other men, and the king said he was heavy, and would fain sleep. Then said Thief: "Get thee home, then, lord, for it better beseemeth men of high estate to lie at home than abroad."

"Nay," said the king, "so will I not do." And he laid him down therewith, and slept fast, snoring loud.

Thief sat close by him, and presently drew his sword from his sheath and cast it far away from him.

A little while after the king woke up, and said: "Was it not so, FRITHIOF, that a many things came into thy mind e'en now? But well hast thou dealt with them, and great honour shalt thou have of me. Lo, now, I knew thee straightway that first evening thou camest into our hall: now nowise speedily shalt thou depart from us; and somewhat great abideth thee."

Said Frithiof: "Lord King, thou hast done to me well, and in friendly wise; but yet must I get me gone soon, because my company cometh speedily to meet me, as I have given them charge to do."

So then they rode home from the wood, and the king's folk came flocking to him, and home they fared to the hall and drank joyously; and it was made known to all folk that Frithiof the Bold had been abiding there through the wintertide.

CHAPTER XIV

KING RING'S GIFT TO FRITHIOF

EARLY of a morning-tide one smote on the door of that hall, wherein slept the king and queen, and many others: then the king asked who it was at the hall door; and so he who was without said: "Here am I, Frithiof; and I am arrayed for my departure."

Then was the door opened, and Frithiof came in, and sang a stave :—

> "Have great thanks for the guesting
> Thou gavest with all bounty;
> Dight fully for wayfaring
> Is the feeder of the eagle;
> But, Ingibiorg, I mind thee
> While yet on earth we tarry;
> Live gloriously! I give thee
> This gift for many kisses."

And therewith he cast the goodly ring towards Ingibiorg, and bade her take it.

The king smiled at this stave of his, and said: "Yea, forsooth, she hath more thanks for thy winter quarters than I; yet hath she not been more friendly to thee than I."

Then sent the king his serving-folk to fetch victuals and drink, and saith that they must eat and drink before Frithiof departed. "So arise, queen, and be joyful!" But she said she was loth to fall a-feasting so early.

"Nay, we will eat all together," said King Ring; and they did so.

But when they had drank a while King Ring spake: "I would that thou abide here, Frithiof; for my sons are but children and I am old, and unmeet for the warding of my realm, if any should bring war against it."

Frithiof said: "Speedily must I be gone, lord." And he sang :—

> " Oh, live, King Ring,
>   Both long and hale!
>   The highest king
>   Neath heaven's skirt!
>   Ward well, O king,
>   Thy wife and land,
>   For Ingibiorg now
>   Never more shall I meet."

Then quoth King Ring :—

> " Fare not away,
>   O Frithiof, thus,
>   With downcast heart,
>   O dearest of chieftains!
>   For now will I give thee
>   For all thy good gifts,
>   Far better things
>   Than thou wottest thyself."

And again he sang :—

> " To Frithiof the famous
> My fair wife I give,
> And all things therewith
> That are unto me."

Then Frithiof took up the word and sang :—

> " Nay, how from thine hands
> These gifts may I have,
> But if thou hast fared
> By the last way of fate ? "

The king said : " I would not give thee this, but that I deem it will soon be so, for I sicken now. But of all men I would that thou shouldst have the joy of this; for thou art the crown of all Norway. The name of king will I give thee also ; and all this, because Ingibiorg's brethren would begrudge thee any honour ; and would be slower in getting thee a wife than I am."

Said Frithiof : " Have all thanks, lord, for thy good-will beyond that I looked for ! but I will have no higher dignity than to be called earl."

Then King Ring gave Frithiof rule over all his realm in due wise, and the name of earl therewith ; and Frithiof was to rule it until such time as the sons of King Ring were of age to rule their own realm. So King Ring lay sick a little while, and then died ; and great mourning was made for him ; then was there a mound cast over him, and much wealth laid therein, according to his bidding.

Thereafter Frithiof made a noble feast, where-unto his folk came; and thereat was drunken at one and the same time the heritage feast after King Ring, and the bridal of Frithiof and Ingibiorg.

After these things Frithiof abode in his realm, and was deemed therein a most noble man; he and Ingibiorg had many children.

CHAPTER XV

FRITHIOF KING IN SOGN

NOW those kings of Sogn, the brethren of Ingibiorg, heard these tidings, how that Frithiof had gotten a king's rule in Ringrealm, and had wedded Ingibiorg their sister. Then says Helgi to Halfdan, his brother, that unheard of it was, and a deed over-bold, that a mere hersir's son should have her to wife: and so thereat they gather together a mighty army, and go their ways therewith to Ringrealm, with the mind to slay Frithiof, and lay all his realm under them.

But when Frithiof was ware of this, he gathered folk, and spake to the queen moreover: "New war is come upon our realm; and now, in whatso wise the dealings go, fain am I that thy ways to me grow no colder."

She said: "In such wise have matters gone that I must needs let thee be the highest."

Now was Biorn come from the east to help Frithiof; so they fared to the fight, and it befell, as ever erst, that Frithiof was the foremost in the peril: King Helgi and he came to handy-blows, and there he slew King Helgi.

Then bade Frithiof raise up the Shield of Peace, and the battle was stayed ; and therewith he cried to King Halfdan : " Two choices are in thine hands now, either that thou give up all to my will, or else gettest thou thy bane like thy brother ; for now may men see that mine is the better part."

So Halfdan chose to lay himself and his realm under Frithiof's sway ; and so now Frithiof became ruler over Sogn-folk, and Halfdan was to be Hersir in Sogn and pay Frithiof tribute, while Frithiof ruled Ringrealm. So Frithiof had the name of King of Sogn-folk from the time that he gave up Ringrealm to the sons of King Ring, and thereafter he won Hordaland also. He and Ingibiorg had two sons, called Gunnthiof and Hunthiof, men of might, both of them.

AND SO HERE ENDETH THE STORY
OF FRITHIOF THE BOLD

THE STORY OF
VIGLUND THE FAIR

THE STORY OF

VIGLUND THE FAIR

CHAPTER I

OF KING HARALD FAIR-HAIR

HARALD Fair-hair, son of Halfdan the Black, was sole King of Norway in the days of this story; and young he was when he gat the kingdom. The wisest of all men was Harald, and well furnished of all prowess that befitted the kingly dignity. The king had a great court, and chose therefor men of fame, even such as were best proven for hardihood and many doughty deeds: and whereas the king was fain to have with him the best men that might be chosen, so also were they held in more account than other men in the land; because the king was niggard to them neither of wealth nor furtherance if they knew how to bear themselves. Nor, on the other hand, did this thing go for little, that none of those who were against the king's will throve ever; for some were driven from the land and some slain; but the king stretched his hand out over all the

wealth they left behind. But many men of
account fled from Norway, and would not bear
the burden of the king, even men of great kin;
for rather would they forego the free lands their
fathers owned, their kin and their friends, than
lie under the thraldom of the king and the hard
days he laid upon them. These went from land
to land; and in those days was Iceland peopled,
for many fled thither who might not abide the
lordship of King Harald.

CHAPTER II

OF OLOF SUNBEAM

THERE was a lord named Thorir, a man of mighty power in Norway, a man of fame, and wedded to a noble wife: this earl begat on his wife a woman-child, Olof by name, who was wondrous fair-mannered from her youth up; and she was the fairest fashioned of all women of Norway, so that her name was lengthened and she was called Olof Sunbeam. The earl loved his daughter much, and was so jealous of her that no son of man might speak with her. He let build a bower for her, and let adorn that house with all kinds of craft. Wide about was it carven and fretted, with gold run through the carving; roofed with lead was this dwelling, and fair bepainted within; round about it was a wall of pales, and therein a wicket iron-bolted strongly: neither was the house adorned in meaner wise without than within.

So in this bower dwelt the earl's daughter, and her serving-women; and the earl sent after those women whom he knew to be most courteous, and let them teach his daughter all the deeds of women which it befitted high-born maidens to know : for the earl had mind, as indeed it came to pass, that his daughter should excel all other women in skill and learning as she did in fairness.

But as soon as she was of age thereto, many noble men fell to wooing her. But the earl was hard to please concerning her, and so it came to pass that he gave her to none, but turned them away with courteous words ; and for her, she mocked none either by word or deed. So slipped away a while and she had the praise of all men.

Now must the tale tell of other folk. There was a man named Ketil, who bare sway over Raum-realm ; he was a mighty man and a wealthy, wise and well befriended. Ketil was wedded, and Ingibiorg was the name of his wife, and she was come of noble blood : two sons they had, Gunnlaug and Sigurd ; bynames had those brethren, for Gunnlaug was called the Masterful, and Sigurd the Sage. Ketil let learn his sons all the craft that it was the wont of those days to learn, for he himself was better furnished with such things than most other men. So the brethren had playmates, and they gave them gold and other good things ; and ever they rode out with their men to shoot the wild things and fowls of the air, for of the greatest prowess and craft were they.

Goodman Ketil was a great fighting man, four-and-twenty holmgangs had he fought, and had won the victory in all.

There was good friendship between King Harald and Ketil.

This Ketil was so great a lawyer, that he never had to do in any case, with whomsoever he dealt, that he did not prevail; for so soon as he began to talk, all folk deemed that so it must be as he said.

The king bade Ketil take a higher dignity, saying, that it well befitted him, both for his wealth's sake and for many other matters; but Ketil would not, and said he had liefer be just a very franklin, and hold himself none the less equal to folk of higher dignity.

Ketil loved his wife so well, that he would not have her know a sorrow.

Thus wore the time away.

CHAPTER III

OF THE SONS OF EARL ERIC

IT befell on a time that King Harald called out
his sea-folk, with the mind to go south along
the land, and arrayed his journey well, both with
ships and men. Ketil got his sons to go with a
very fair company in the king's fellowship, but
he himself sat at home, for he was now sunken
into eld.

Now when the king was ready he sailed south
along the land; but when he came south to
Rogaland, there was an earl held sway there called
Eric; a great chieftain, and well beloved of his
men: who, when he heard of the king's coming,
let array a fair feast and bade the king thereto
with all his company; that the king took, and
went ashore with his host, and the earl led him
home to his hall, with all his court and all kinds
of minstrelsy and songs and harp-playing, and
every disport that might be. With such welcom-
ing the earl brought the king to his hall, and set
him in the high seat, and there befell the fairest
feast, and the king was exceeding joyous, and all
his men, because the earl spared in nought to

serve the king with all loving-kindness; and the
best of drink was borne forth, and men were
speedily merry with drink.

The king ever set Ketil's sons beside him, and
they had great honour of him: the earl stood
before the king, and served himself at his board,
and great grew the glee in the hall. Then the
king caused those brethren to pour out, and set
the earl in the high seat beside him; and the
brethren did straightway as the king bade, and
gat great praise of men for their courtesy. But
when the boards were taken up, the earl let bear
forth good things which he had chosen for the
king, yea, and to all his men he gave some good
gift or other; and at the end of this gift-giving
the earl let bear forth a harp, whose strings were
this one of gold and that one of silver, and the
fashion of it most glorious; and the king stretched
forth his hand to meet it, and began to smite it;
and so great and fair a voice had this harp, that
all wondered, and thought they had never heard
the like before.

Then spake the earl: "I would, lord, that
thou wentest with me for thy disport, and then
will I show thee all I have, within and without,
and both cornfield and orchard."

So the king did as the earl bade, and went and
beheld all about, and made much of it; and they
came to a certain apple-orchard wherein was a
fair grove, and under the grove three lads a-playing: fair were they all, but one much the most
fair. So they sat a-playing at tables, and that

one played against the twain; then these deemed
that their game was coming to nought before
him, and so they cast the board together; thereat
was the better one wroth, and he smote each of
them with his fist: then they fell to and wrestled,
the two against him alone, and he prevailed no
less in the wrestling than in the table-play.

Then the earl bade them forbear and be at one,
and they did so, and played at tables as before.
And the king and his company went home to
the hall, and sat them down; and it was well
seen of the king that he thought much of that
youngling; and he asked the earl concerning what
those lads were.

"They are my sons," said the earl.

"Are they of one mother?" said the king.

"Nay," said the earl.

Then the king asked what they hight, and the
earl said, "Sigmund and Helgi, but Thorgrim is
the third, and love-born is he."

So a little after came all those brethren into
the hall, and Thorgrim went the hindermost; for
in this, as in other matters, was he less honoured.

The earl called the boys to him, and bade them
go before the king; and they did so, and greeted
him: but when they came before him, Thorgrim
put a hand on each of his brethren, and pushed
them from him, and passed forth betwixt them,
and stood up on the footpace and greeted the
king, and kissed him: but the king laughed and
took the lad, and set him down beside him, and
asked him of his mother; but he said he was the

sister's son of Hersir Thorir of Sogn. Then the
king pulled a gold ring off his arm, and gave it
to Thorgrim.

Then Thorgrim went back to his brethren, and
the feast endured with the greatest honour till
the king declared his will to depart.

"Now," said he, "because of the great-hearted-
ness thou hast shown to me, shalt thou thyself
choose thy reward."

The earl was glad thereat, and said, that he
would have the king take Thorgrim his son to
him: "Better," saith he, "do I deem that than
store of pennies, because that everything that
thou wouldst do to me, I shall deem so much
the better if thou doest it to him; and for that
cause am I fain he should go with thee, because
I love him the best of all my sons."

So the king said yea thereto, and departed, and
Thorgrim with him, who right soon grew to be
most gentle of manner in all service to the king;
wherefore began many of the king's men to envy
him.

CHAPTER IV

THORGRIM WOOETH OLOF SUNBEAM

THE tale tells, that on a time the king went a-guesting to a man named Sigurd, and the feast was well arrayed with all things needful : and the king bade Thorgrim stand forth that day, and pour out for him and his chosen friends. Now many men misliked the great honour in which the king held Thorgrim : and Sigurd had a kinsman called Grim, a man wealthy of money ; a man of such dignity, that he accounted all men nought beside him : this man was at the feast, and sat on the daïs at the higher bench. So Thorgrim served that day ; and as he bare a great beaker of drink before Grim, the liquor was spilt out of it because Thorgrim stumbled, and it fell on Grim's raiment. He grew wroth thereat, and sprang up with big words, saying, that it was well seen that the son of a whore was more wont to herding swine, and giving them their wash, than to serving any men of account.

Thorgrim waxed wroth at his words, and drew his sword and thrust him through, and men pulled him dead from under the board. Then

Sigurd called on his men and bade them stand up
and lay hands on Thorgrim : but the king said :
" Nay, Sigurd, do it not ! for Grim should fall
unatoned because of his word ; yet will I atone
him with a full weregild, if thou wilt that I deal
with the matter as I will : for thus will our friendship be better holden."

So it must be as the king would, and he paid
so much money that Sigurd was well content ; and
the feast wore away, and there is nought more to
tell of it.

Then the king went his ways home : and now
he bade the great men to him, and first of these
Earl Thorir, and Master Ketil of Raum-realm ;
who now lacked a wife, because Ingibiorg had
died in child-bed, when she had born a daughter,
who was called Ingibiorg after her mother : but
after these the king bade many men and a great
company, for there was no lack of all things
needful.

So men came as they were bidden to the feast ;
and Olof Sunbeam came thereto with her father.
So men were marshalled to their seats and noble
drink was borne forth.

Thorgrim went a-serving, and folk heeded
much what a sprightly and goodly man he was :
he was seemly clad, for the king honoured him
exceedingly, and that misliked many of his men,
and they hated Thorgrim therefor ; and a byname
was given him, and he was called Thorgrim the
Proud.

But when Thorgrim saw Olof his heart yearned

toward her, and even so it fared with her toward
him, for she loved him; but folk noted it not,
though as time served them they met together,
and either was well-liking to other: so Thorgrim
asked her how she would answer if he bade her
in wedlock; and she said that for her part she
would not gainsay it, if her father would have it
so. So at the end of the feast Thorgrim set
forth his wooing and craved Olof Sunbeam.
Earl Thorir was not swift in assenting thereto,
and they parted with so much done.

CHAPTER V

THE WEDDING OF OLOF SUNBEAM

A LITTLE after Thorgrim gat speech of the king, and craved leave to go see Earl Thorir, and the king granted the same; and when Thorgrim came to Earl Thorir's he had good welcome there.

Then again Thorgrim fell to his wooing, and would now know for sure what answer the earl would give; but the earl said he would not wed his daughter to him.

Thorgrim was there three nights, and he and Olof met lovingly; and some folk say that at that tide they plighted their troth. And so Thorgrim went back to the king for that time.

Now he went on warfare, and was fully come to man's estate; so he was a-warring through the summer, and was accounted the stoutest of men in all dangers, and he gat to him in this journey both riches and renown.

But after these things it befell that Ketil of Raumarik came a-riding to Earl Thorir's with thirty men, and King Harald also was a-guesting there. Then Ketil fell a-wooing Olof Sunbeam

to wed her, and with the furtherance of the king
Earl Thorir gave his daughter Olof to Ketil : but
Olof neither said yea thereto nor thought it in
her heart : and when the betrothals were to be
fulfilled she sang a stave :—

> " Sure glad ring-warder singeth
> Sweeter than any other ;
> O Voice amid Earth's voices
> Henceforth but woe unto me !
> No ring-warder so white is
> That he may win look from me :
> One man have I made oath for,
> And well beloved is he."

Now most men held it for sooth that Olof
had been fain to wed Thorgrim, but it behoved
to go the other way.

So the day was appointed whereon the wedding was to be, and that was at winter-nights
in the house of Earl Thorir : so wore away the
summer.

But in the autumn came Thorgrim back from
warfare, and heard that Olof was betrothed ; so
he went straightway to the king, and craved
help of him to get the woman, whether Earl
Thorir liked it better or worse, or Ketil either.
But the king utterly gainsayed all help to Thorgrim, saying that Ketil was his best friend.

"And I will give thee this counsel," said the
king, "that thou raise no strife with Ketil : I
will woo Ingibiorg his daughter for thee, and
in such wise shall ye make good peace between
you !"

Thorgrim said he would not have it so: "I will hold," says he, "to my words, and the oaths that Olof and I swore betwixt us; and her will I have or no woman else. And since thou wilt help me not, I will serve thee no longer."

Said the king: "Thou must even rule the matter as thou wilt; but methinks it is most like that thy honour shall wax no greater in another place than with me."

So Thorgrim took leave of the king, and the king gave him a gold ring at parting which weighed a mark; and so he went to his own men.

Now it lacked three nights of the wedding-day; so Thorgrim went up a-land alone for any of his own men, and went till he came to the house of Earl Thorir.

Thither he came by then that the bride was set on the bench, and all the drinking-hall was full of men, and the king was set in the high-seat, and the feast was at its full height.

So Thorgrim went into the drinking-hall, yea, unto the midst of the floor, and stood there; and so many lights were there in the hall, that no shadow fell from aught. All men knew Thorgrim, and to many, forsooth, he was no unwelcome guest.

So he spake: "Hast thou, Ketil, wooed and won Olof?"

Ketil said that so it was.

"Was it aught with her assent?" said he.

Says Ketil: "I am minded to think that Earl

Thorir might give his daughter away himself, and that the match so made would be lawful forsooth."

"This is my word," says Thorgrim, "that Olof and I have sworn oath each to each that she should have no man but me. Let her say if it be so."

And Olof said it was true.

"Then meseemeth the woman is mine," said Thorgrim.

"Thou shalt never have her," said Ketil. "I have striven with greater men than thou, and prevailed against them."

Said Thorgrim: "Well, meseems thou dost these things in trust of the king's furtherance; so here I bid thee to holm. Let us fight it out, and he shall have the woman who winneth her on holm."

"Nay, I am minded to make the most of it that I have more men than thou," said Ketil.

But lo, while they were a-talking thus, all lights died out throughout the hall, and there was mighty uproar and jostling; but when lights were brought again the bride was gone, and Thorgrim withal; and all men deemed it clear that he had brought it about: and true it was that Thorgrim had taken the bride and brought her to his ship. His men had made all ready even as he had aforetime appointed them, and now they were arrayed for sea; so they hoisted sail as soon as Thorgrim was ready, for the wind blew from off the land.

These things befell in the thick of the land-settling-time of Iceland; and Thorgrim thought sure enough that he might not hold himself in Norway after this business: so he made for Iceland. They put forth into the sea and had a fair wind, and made Snowfellness, and went a-land at Hraunhaven.

But the king and the earl heard of Thorgrim's journey, and Ketil was deemed to have won the greatest shame, in that he had lost his wife, and it was not well seen that he would have right of Thorgrim. The king made Thorgrim an outlaw for this deed at Ketil's urging: but turn we from these a while.

CHAPTER VI

OF KETILRID AND HER KIN

THERE was a man named Holmkel, who dwelt at Foss on Snowfellness, by Holmkel's River : he had to wife Thorbiorg, the daughter of Einar of Bath-brent, and they had two sons together, one named Jokul and the other Einar. Holmkel was the son of Alfarin, who was the son of Vali; his brothers were Ingiald of Ingialdsknoll, and Hauskuld of Hauskuldstead, and Goti of Gotisbrook.

So Thorgrim the Proud bought the lands of Ingialdsknoll, and Ingiald on the other hand went a-trading, and comes not into our tale. Thorgrim soon became a great chieftain, and a most bounteous man ; and he got to be great friends with Holmkel of Foss.

Now tells the tale that he made a wedding for Olof, and the winter after they set up house at Ingialdsknoll Olof bore a child, a man-child that had to name Trusty; the next winter she bore another boy, who was called Viglund, and he soon grew both strong and fair.

The same year Thorbiorg bore a woman-child,

and it was named Ketilrid; so she and Viglund were of an age: but Trusty was one winter older.

So they grew up in that country, and all would be saying thereabout that there was neither man nor maid of fairer promise or of better conditions in all things than were Viglund and Ketilrid.

Holmkel loved his daughter so much that he would do nought against her will, but Thorbiorg loved her little.

Now whenas Viglund was ten and Trusty eleven winters old, there were none of that age as strong as they in all the country side, and Viglund was the stronger; their other conditions were according to this, and moreover Thorgrim spared in nought to teach his sons.

But Thorbiorg of Foss would learn her daughter no skill, and Holmkel thought it great pity of that; so he took the rede at last to ride to Ingialdsknoll with his daughter; and Thorgrim greeted him well, for great was the friendship between them. Holmkel was seeking fostering there for his daughter with Olof, that she might teach her skill, for Olof was accounted the most skilled of all women of Iceland; she took her rejoicing and got to love her exceeding well.

By this had Olof a young daughter named Helga, a year younger than Ketilrid; and so these young folk drew together in all joyance and glee: but in all games betwixt them it ever so befell that Viglund and Ketilrid would fall into company together, and the brother and sister Trusty and Helga. And now great love grew up between

Viglund and Ketilrid, and many would be saying
that it would make an even match for many causes.
But ever when they were together would either
gaze at other and turn to nought else. And on a
time Viglund spoke and said that he was fain they
should bind their love with oath and troth; but
Ketilrid was slow thereover.

Said she: " There are many things against it:
first, that thou mayest not be in the same mind when
thou art fully come to man's estate; for about
such things are ye men's minds nought steadfast.
And again, it is not meet, neither will I have it,
that we go against my father's counsels herein.
And a third thing I see that may fret it all away
is, that I am of no might in my matters; for so
it is that these things go mostly after my mother's
will, and she has little love for me: yet, indeed, I
know none that I would rather have than thee, if
I might rule matters; but my heart tells me that
troubles great and sore lie in the way of it, however it may be in the end."

Full oft got Viglund's talk on to the same road,
and ever she answered in like wise; and yet men
deem indeed that they must have sworn troth each
to each.

CHAPTER VII

THOSE BRETHREN OF FOSS COME TO INGIALDSKNOLL

NOW must we tell of the brethren Jokul and Einar, how they became exceeding ill-ruled in the country-side, treading herein in the foot-steps of their mother. Holmkel was ill-content therewith, but might not better it, and they got to be hated because of their goings on.

Now on a time Einar fell to speech with his mother, and said : " I am ill-content with the honour Thorgrim the Proud has in the country-side ; and I am minded to try if I may not do my will on Olof his wife ; and then it would either be that he would strive to avenge it, or else would his honour lie alow : neither is it all so sure that he would get the better of it, if he strove to get the thing avenged."

She said it was well spoken and just her very mind. So on a certain day, when Holmkel was from home, rode Einar to Ingialdsknoll, and Jokul his brother with him.

Olof the good-wife had bidden a home-woman of hers to lock the men's door every morning

K

whenas the men were gone to work; and in such
wise did she the morning those twain came to the
stead.   So the home-woman was ware of their
coming, and went to Olof's bedchamber and told
her that the Foss-dwellers were come thither.   So
Olof arose and clad herself, and went to her sewing-
bower, and set down on the daïs there a hand-
maiden, casting her own mantle over her, and
saying: "Take it nought strange though they
think thee to be me, and I shall look to it that
thou get no shame of them."

Therewith she sent another home-woman to the
door, for there was no man in the house.   So
Einar asked where Olof was, and it was told him
that she was in her sewing-bower.   Thither turned
both those brethren, and when they came into
the chamber, they beheld how Olof sat on the
daïs; so Einar sat down by her and began his
talk with her.

But therewith came one into the hall clad in
blue and with a drawn sword in hand, not great
of growth, but exceeding wroth of aspect.

They asked of his name, and he called himself
Ottar; they knew him not, and yet they waxed
somewhat adrad of the man.

Now he took up the word and spake: "All
must out, and welcome home Thorgrim the goodman, who is a-riding to the garth."   Then up
sprang the brethren, and went out, and beheld
where the goodman rode with a great company;
so they leapt on their horses and rode away home.

But it turned out that that great company was

but the beasts being driven home; yea, and the blue-clad man was even Olof herself: and when the Foss-folk knew that, they thought their journey but pitiful: so ever waxed great hatred betwixt the houses.

But when goodman Thorgrim came home Olof told him all that was befallen, and he spake: "Let us tell nought hereof abroad, because of Holmkel my friend: for Einar did it not with his consenting."

CHAPTER VIII

OF A HORSEFIGHT

NOW those brethren had a stallion, brown of colour and a savage beast; every horse he dealt with he drave away : and two tusks he had, so huge that they were like no teeth of horses. Viglund also had a stallion, light-dun of colour, the best and fairest of horses, and held of great account amongst them. Thorgrim the Proud withal had two oxen, blaze-faced, and with horns like polished bone, and these oxen he liked well.

Now on a day the brethren Einar and Jokul rode to Ingialdsknoll, and there found the father and sons all three standing without the door : so Jokul asked Viglund to give him his light-dun horse. Viglund said he had scarce made up his mind to that; then said Jokul that it was niggardly done : but Viglund said he took no keep thereof.

"Then let us fight the horses," said Jokul.

"That meseems maybe," quoth Viglund.

"And that," said Jokul, "I deem better than the gift of thine to me."

"Good," says Viglund; "let the thing go as it will."

Therewith they appoint a day for the horse-fight. So when the day was came the brown of those brethren was led forth, and devilish was his demeanour; so both the brethren got ready to follow him. Then in came Viglund's light-dun, and when he came into the ring he went about circling, till he reared up and smote both his forefeet on the brown's muzzle so that the tusks were driven from out him; thereafter he made at the brown with his teeth, and smote him in the belly, and tore him through, and the brown fell down dead. But when the Foss-folk saw that, they ran to their weapons, and so did the others, and there they fought till Holmkel and Thorgrim gat them parted; and by then was fallen one man of Viglund's, but two of the brethren's men; and in such wise men departed.

But still held the friendship between Holmkel and Thorgrim; and Holmkel withal got to know of the love between Ketilrid and Viglund, and did nought to hinder it: but Thorbiorg and her sons were exceeding ill-content therewith.

So wore away the time, till it was the talk of all men, that none of that day in Iceland were as fair as Viglund and Ketilrid, or as good in all skill and courtesy.

CHAPTER IX

EVIL DEEDS OF THOSE BRETHREN

THE tale tells, that on a time those brethren,
Einar and Jokul, went from home a night-
tide when it was bright and clear, and came to
the fell-common whereas dwelt Viglund's light-
dun : they went up to the horses and would drive
them home, but might not in anywise, for the
dun warded the horses from their driving, but
they had been minded to drive all the horses
about him to impound him.

So when they might not bring it about they
waxed exceeding wroth, and set on the stallion
with weapons to slay him; but he defended himself with hoofs and teeth so mightily, that the
night was far spent and nothing done: but it
came to pass in the end that they got within
spear-thrust of him and slew him so.

But when they had done it they were loth to
drive the horses home, for they deemed that then
it would be clearly seen that they had slain the
stallion, and they were fain to hide the same; so
they dragged him over a shear rock, with the
intent that it should be thought that he had

tumbled over of himself: then they fared home, and made as if nought had happened.

Again a little after went the brethren Einar and Jokul to a hill-common of Thorgrim the Proud wherein went his gelded beasts : and there had he a herd of fifty oxen.

So the brethren knew the goodly blaze-faced oxen, and took them and cast halters over them and led them along to Foss, and there slew them both, and then went and hung them up in an out-house. This was a-night time, and they had made an end of their work before the home-men arose.

Their mother knew all about it, and was, for-sooth, exceeding busy in helping her sons over this work of theirs.

CHAPTER X

HOLMKEL RIDES TO INGIALDSKNOLL

NOW must it be told, how that the brethren, Viglund and Trusty, went one day to their horses; and when they came to the hill-common to them, they missed their stallion, and, seeking him far and wide, found him at last stark dead under a great cliff; many and great wounds they found on him, and he had been thrust clean through.

So Viglund and his brother thought it clear that the Foss-folk had done it; so they went home and told how their horse was dead, and how it must have been done by the Foss-folk.

Thorgrim bade them keep it quiet; says he, "They were the first to lose their horse; and ye will have your turn again, if things go as I deem, even though ye let this pass over."

So for that time they let it pass at first: but not long after Thorgrim was told that his goodly blaze-faced oxen were gone, even those that he held in most account, and withal that folk deemed it the work of men.

Thorgrim made few words thereover, but said

that it was most like that thieves who dwelt abroad in the mountains would have done such a deed ; neither did he let any search be made for the oxen.

So this was heard far and wide, and men deemed that those of Ingialdsknoll had great scathe hereby.

Thorbiorg of Foss made plentiful mocking about this, and let eat the slaughtered oxen : but when goodman Holmkel came to know where the oxen were gotten to, he takes his horse and rides off to Ingialdsknoll : but when he finds goodman Thorgrim he tells him that he thinks his goodly oxen have gotten to his house, and that his sons must have done it. " And now," says he, " I will pay for the oxen out and out, even as much as thou thyself wilt, if thou bring not their guilt home to them by law."

Thorgrim says that so it shall be ; and so he took as much money as made him well content, and he and Holmkel parted with great friendship.

CHAPTER XI

THE BREWING OF A WITCH-STORM

A WOMAN named Kiolvor dwelt at Hraun-
skard, a great witch-wife of very ill conditions and hateful to all folk; and there was great
friendship between her and Thorbiorg of Foss.
So the mother and sons, Thorbiorg to wit, Einar
and Jokul, bargained with Kiolvor and gave her
a hundred in silver, so that she should overcome
those brethren, Viglund and Trusty, by some
such manner of witchcraft as she might see her
way to. For the greatest envy beat about the
hearts of these; and they had heard withal of the
true love of Viglund and Ketilrid, and grudged
that they should have joy one of the other, as
was well proven afterwards.

But they twain loved ever hotter and hotter,
with secret love and desire enfolded in their
breasts, even from the time they first grew up;
so that the roots of love and the waxing of desire
were never torn up from the hearts of them;
even as the nature of love is, that the fire of
longing and flame of desire burneth ever the hotter, and knitteth the more together the breast and

heart of the lovers, as folk stand more in the way thereof, as kith and kin cast greater hindrances before those betwixt whom sweet love and yearning lieth. Even so it fared with these folk, Viglund and Ketilrid; for ever all the days while they both lived they loved so hotly, that neither might look away from the other, from the time they first looked each on each, if they might but do as their hearts' yearning was.

Now there was a man named Biorn, a home-man of Thorgrim the Proud, and he was called Biorn of the Billows, because he was such a sea-dog that he deemed no weather unmeet to put to sea in; and he would ever say that he heeded nought the idle tricks of the billows. He had come out with Thorgrim, and his business it was to look to his craft; and there was good fishing off the ness. He never rowed out with more than two men, though he had a stout ten-oared yawl; but now this autumn it befell by Kiolvor's witch-craft that both his fellows lay sick, and all men else were busy about the hay. So Biorn would row a-fishing, wherefore he bade Viglund and Trusty go with him that day. They did so, because the weather was fair, and they all good friends together. But Kiolvor knew all this, and went up on to her witch-house, and waved her veil out toward the east quarter, and thereby the weather grew thick speedily.

So when they were gotten on to the fishing-banks there was fish enough under them, till they beheld how a cloud-fleck came up from the east

and north-east. Then said Viglund : "Meseems
it were good to make for land, for I like not the
look of the weather."

Says Biorn : "Nay, let us wait till the ship is
laden."

"Thou shalt be master," said Viglund.

Therewith the cloud-fleck drew all over the
sky, and brought with it both wind and frost,
and such an ill sea, that the waters were nowhere
still, but drave about like grains of salt.

And now Biorn said they would make for land.
"Better before," said Viglund ; "but I will say
nought against it now." So Biorn and Trusty
rowed, and made no way forward ; but they drove
south-west out to sea ; and the craft began to fill
under them.

Then Viglund bade Biorn bale and Trusty
steer, but he himself took the oars, and rowed so
mightily that they made land at Daymealness.
There dwelt Thorkel Skinhood, who came out
with Bardi the Snowfell-sprite, and was now old.

Now when it was told Ketilrid that they had
been driven out to sea and were dead, she fell
into a faint ; but when she came to herself she
sang this stave as she looked out toward the sea. :

No   more now   may   my   ey - en

meet   the   sea   un - greet - ing,

Since the day my speech - friend

sank be - low the sea - banks.

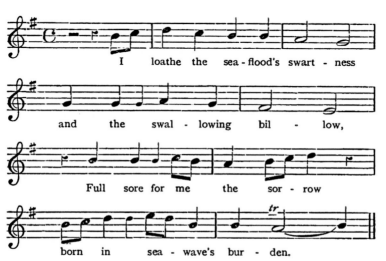

I loathe the sea - flood's swart - ness

and the swal - lowing bil - low,

Full sore for me the sor - row

born in sea - wave's bur - den.

But Thorkel gave the brethren a good welcome, and the next day they went home; and sweet and joyful was the meeting betwixt Viglund and Ketilrid.

CHAPTER XII

OF HAKON THE EAST-MAN

NOW must we take up the story whereas we left it awhile agone; for Ketil Ram was ill-content with such an ending of his case with Thorgrim the Proud; but he was fast getting old now, and he deemed it not easy to get aught done. His sons Sigurd and Gunnlaug were become hardy men and goodly, and Ingibiorg his daughter was the fairest of all women.

Now there was a man named Hakon, a Wickman of kin, wealthy and warlike: this man went his ways to Ketil of Raum-realm, and craved his daughter in wedlock; and Ketil gave this answer to his asking: "I will give thee my daughter on these wise; thou wilt first fare out to Iceland and slay Thorgrim the Proud, and bring me the head of him."

Hakon said he thought that no great matter; and so they struck the bargain. Hakon fared to Iceland that summer, and brought his ship into Frodaroyce; and the Foss-folk Jokul and Einar came first to the ship: the ship-master gave them good welcome, and asked them many things; and they were free of tidings to him.

Then he asked concerning lodging, and they said there was none better than at their father's house at Foss.

"A sister we have," said they, "so fair and courteous, that her like is not to be found; and we will do for thee which thou wilt; either give her to thee as a wife, or let thee have her as a concubine: so come, we bid thee thither to guest with us."

The master thought this a thing to be desired, so he said he would go thither; and tells them withal what errand he had in Iceland; and they liked the thing well: and now all bind themselves as fellows in the plot.

A little after went the ship-master home to Foss; forsooth clean against the will of Holmkel the goodman: but so it had to be. In a little while withal the ship-master got to be great friends with Thorbiorg; for he gave her many goodly things.

So on a time this Hakon fell to talk with the mother and sons, and asked where the woman was whereof the brethren had told him; "for I would see her," says he.

They said she was being fostered with Olof at Ingialdsknoll; so he bade them see to it and have her home: "For," said he, "I trust full well to have thy furtherance in the getting of my will of her, because of our friendship."

So a little after this Thorbiorg fell a-talking with goodman Holmkel. "I will," she said, "that my daughter Ketilrid come home to me."

"Well," said the goodman, "I deem it better that she be left in peace where she is gotten to."

"Nay, it shall not be," says she; "rather will I go fetch her myself, than that she should have such rumour from Viglund as now lieth on her: yea, I will rather wed her to Hakon; for that methinks were a seemly match."

Therewith they make an end of talking; and Holmkel thought he could see, that Thorbiorg would send after Ketilrid, and he deems it better to go fetch her himself. So he rode to Ingialds-knoll, and had good welcome there.

But when he was come thither Viglund went to Ketilrid and spake thus with her: "Thy father is come hither; and methinks he is come after thee to bring thee home with him, and he must needs have his will. But now, Ketilrid, I am full fain that thou keep in memory all the privy talk we have had together, for indeed I know that thou wilt never be out of my mind."

Then said Ketilrid, sore weeping: "Long have I seen that we might not long have this joy in peace; and now belike it were better that we had not said so much: but not all so sure it is that thou lovest me better than I love thee; though my words be less than thine. But now herein do I see the redes of my mother; because for a long while I have had but little love of her; and most like it is that the days of our bliss are over and done if she may have her will of me: nevertheless should I be well content if I wist that all went well with thee. But howsoever it be, we shall never come together in bliss, but if the will of my father prevail; and a heavy yoke he has to drive, whereas my mother and brothers are afield, for in all things will they be against me. But thou, let all these things slip from off thee!"

Then went Viglund to Ketilrid and kissed her; and it was easily seen of her, yea and of both of them, how hard it was for them to part as at that time.

Moreover, Viglund sang a stave:—

"Young now I shall not ever
Love any silken goddess,
That son of man shall say it,
Save thee alone, O Sweetling!
Therefore fair maid remember
The oath we swore aforetime,
Howso that woman wilful
Would waste the love between us."

Then Ketilrid went into the house to her father, who straightway told her that she must away home with him. Ketilrid says that he must have his will; "But good," says she, "would I deem it to abide here ever: yet must it be even as it must."

A great matter it was to all to part with Ketilrid, for she was a joy to the heart of every man.

But now they ride home to Foss: and the ship-master was wondrous fain of her coming home: but Thorbiorg her mother appointed her to serve Hakon; which thing she would in nowise do,

L

but told her father thereof weeping ; and he said :
"Thou shalt not serve Hakon but if thou wilt :
yea that alone shalt thou do which thou willest,
and thou shalt be by me both day and night."

She said she was right glad of that : and so the
time wore away a space, in such wise that Hakon
got never a word with her.

CHAPTER XIII

BALL-PLAY ON ESJA-TARN

NOW was ball-play set up on Esja-tarn, and the Foss-men were the setters forth of the sport : and the first day when men came home from these games, Ketilrid asked if none had come thither from Ingialdsknoll; and she was told that they had all been there, both the father and sons, and Olof and her daughter Helga : so Ketilrid craved of her father next day that she might go to the play; he said yea thereto; and so they went all together that day, and great was the glee : for Thorgrim's sons were come and none other from Ingialdsknoll.

So the brethren went up on to the bank whereas the women sat; and Ketilrid stood up to meet them, and greeted them lovingly, and they sat down on either hand of her, Viglund and Trusty.

Then spake Ketilrid : "Now will I be just as kind to one of you as the other, and hoodwink folk thereby."

Therewith she gazed ever on Viglund and said : "Thy name will I lengthen this day, and call thee

Viglund the FAIR: and this ring I will give thee, which my father gave me as a toothing-token, and it shall be to thee a naming-token."

So he took the ring and drew it on to his hand; and gave her again the ring Harald's-gift, for his father had given it to him. And so, long was their talk drawn out: but when the Foss-men saw that, they took it sore to heart.

So either fare home that evening; and Hakon fell to speech with Thorbiorg, and bade her forbid her daughter to go to any more such meetings of men-folk, in such a mood as she was. She assented thereto, and told Holmkel the goodman not to let his daughter go to any play; but let her abide at home in peace rather: and he did so, and Ketilrid's gladness departed from her. Then her father said, she should be ever by him at home if she thought it better so; and she said it pleased her well.

But men go to the play as aforetime; and one had one side, one the other in the play, the Foss-folk and Thorgrim's sons. And on a time Viglund drave the ball out beyond Jokul. Jokul waxed wroth thereat, and when he got the ball, he took it and drave it into Viglund's face, so hard that the skin of his brow fell down over his eyes. Then Trusty ripped a rag from his shirt, and bound up his brother's brow, and when that was done the Foss-folk were departed.

So the brethren went home; and when they came into the hall, Thorgrim cried out as he sat · on the daïs, "Welcome, dear son and daughter!"

" Why dost thou make women of us, father ? "
said Trusty.

" Belike," said Thorgrim, " a coif-wearer should
be a woman."

" No woman am I," said Viglund.   " Yet mayhappen I am not so far short of it."

" Why didst thou not pay Jokul back ? " said
Thorgrim.

" They were gone," said Trusty, " by then I
had bound up his face."   And so the talk came
to an end.

The next day both the brethren went to the
play; and so when it was least to be looked for,
Viglund drave the ball right into Jokul's face, so
that the skin burst.   Then Jokul went to smite
Viglund with his bat, but Viglund ran in under
the blow and cast Jokul down on the ice, so that
he lay long swooning ; and therewith were they
parted, and either side went home.   Jokul had
no might to get a-horseback, and was borne home
betwixt the four corners of a cloth : but he
mended speedily, and the play was set up at Foss.
So Thorgrim's sons arrayed them for the play.
Thorgrim would have stayed them, saying that
he deemed sore troubles would come of it ; but
they went none the less.

So when they came into the hall at Foss the
play was begun, but folk were all in their seats
in the hall.   So Viglund went in and up to the
daïs, whereon sat the goodman and his daughter ;
and Ketilrid greeted him well.

He took her up from her seat, and sat himself

down therein, and set her on his knee. But when the goodman saw that, he edged away and gave place, and then Ketilrid sat her down between them, and they fell to talk together.

Then let the goodman get them a pair of tables, and there they played daylong.

Hakon was ill at ease at that; and ever that winter had he been talking to goodman Holmkel and craving his daughter; but Holmkel answered ever in one wise, and said it might not be.

So wore the day till the brethren got them ready to go; but when they were on the causeway, lo, Ketilrid was in the path before them, and bade them not fare home that night. "Because," quoth she, "I know that my brethren will waylay you."

But Viglund said he would go as he had been minded afore, and they did so; and each of them had his axe in his hand. But when they came to a certain stackgarth, lo the Foss-folk, twelve in company.

Then said Jokul: "Good that we have met, Viglund; now shall I pay thee back for stroke of ball and felling on the ice."

"I have nought to blame my luck herein," said Viglund.

So they fell on the two brethren, who defended themselves well and manly. Viglund fought no great while before he had slain a man, and then another, and Trusty slew a third.

Then said Jokul: "Now let us hold our hands, and lay all these feuds on those brethren."

So did they, and either side went their ways home ; and Jokul tells his father that Viglund and Trusty had slain three of his home-men. "But we," quoth he, "would do nought against them till we had seen thee."

Now Holmkel was exceeding wroth at this tale.

CHAPTER XIV

KETILRID BETROTHED TO HAKON

JOKUL kept on egging his father to wed Ketilrid his daughter to Hakon; so, what with the urging of those brethren, Holmkel did betroth her to him, but utterly against her will. Hakon was well minded to abide in Iceland, whereas he saw he could not bring to pass the slaying of Thorgrim the Proud.

So this was heard of at Ingialdsknoll, and Viglund took it much to heart.

But when Holmkel knew the very sooth about the waylaying of the brethren, he deemed he had done overmuch in giving Ketilrid to Hakon.

Now still came the sons of Thorgrim to the games at Foss as heretofore; and Viglund had speech of Ketilrid, and blamed her much with hard words in that she was betrothed. But when they arrayed them to go that night, lo, Hakon had vanished, and the sons of Holmkel, and many others with them. Then spake the goodman with Viglund: "I would," said he, "that ye went not home to-night: for meseemeth the departure of those brethren looks untrustworthy."

But Viglund said he would go, as he had afore been minded : but when they came out a-doors, there was Ketilrid in the way before them, who prayed Viglund to go another road. "No great things will I do for thy word," said he; and he sang withal :—

> " Stem where the gathered gold meets,
>   All trust I gave unto thee :
>   Last thought of all thoughts was it
>   That thou couldst wed another.
>   But now no oaths avail us,
>   Nought are our many kisses ;
>   Late learn we of women :—
>   Her word to me is broken."

"I think not that I have done any such thing," said Ketilrid; "but indeed I would that thou wentest not!"

"It shall not be," said Viglund; "for I have more mind to try the matter out with Hakon, than to let him cast his arms about thee, while I am alive to see it." And he sang :—

> " I would abide the bale-fire,
>   Or bear the steel-tree's smiting,
>   As other men may bear it ;
>   But heavy maidens' redes are :
>   Sorely to me it seemeth,
>   Gold spoilers' shoulder-branches,
>   The sweet that was my maiden
>   Other than mine entwining."

CHAPTER XV

THE BATTLE OF THE FOSS-FOLK AND THORGRIM'S SONS

SO they went on their way till they came to the stackgarth, whereas they had had to do before: and there were the Foss-folk, twelve in company.

Then the sons of Thorgrim gat them up on to the hay, which was in the garth, so that the others were not ware of them, till they had torn up great store of the frozen turf.

But when they had so done, they saw Thorgrim's sons, and fell on them, and there befell the fiercest of fights: till the Foss-folk saw that they made way slowly against Thorgrim's sons whiles they were up on the hay: then cried Jokul—

"Thou wert well counselled, Viglund, not to slink away; and we shall hold for certain that thou art no good man and true, but if thou come down from the hay there, and try the matter to its end."

So, because of Jokul's egging on, Viglund leapt down from the hay with Trusty his brother, and they met fiercely; and all the men of Hakon and

those brethren fell, so that of the Foss-dwellers
these alone stood on their feet, Jokul, Einar, and
Hakon, with two men more who were hurt and
unmeet for fight.

Thus said Jokul: "Now let us set to work in
manly and generous wise; let Trusty and Einar
fight together, and Viglund and Hakon, and I
will sit beside the while."

Now Trusty was both sore and weary; and they
fought, Trusty and Einar, till either fell.

Then fell to fight Viglund and Hakon; and
Viglund was exceeding weary, but unwounded.

The fight was both hard and long, because
Hakon was strong and stout-hearted, but Viglund
strong of hand, and skilled in arms and eager of
heart : but the end of their dealings was, that
Hakon fell dead to earth, while Viglund was sore
hurt.

Then up sprung Jokul, fresh, and without a
hurt, and turned against Viglund, and they fell
to fight : and a long space they fought, and
hard enow, till none could see which would win
the day; when Viglund sees that it is a hard
matter to prevail against Jokul to the end because
of his wounds and weariness; and so being as
good with one hand as the other, he cast aloft
axe and shield, and caught his shield with his
right hand and his axe with his left, in such wise
that Jokul noted it not, and then smote the
right arm from off him at the crook of the
elbow. Then Jokul took to flight, nor might
Viglund follow after him; but he caught up a

spear from the ground, whereas many lay beside him, and cast it after Jokul; and that spear smote him, and went in at the shoulders and out at the breast of him; and Jokul fell down dead.

But Viglund was grown faint with the flow of blood, and he fell swooning and lay there as one dead.

Then the two Foss-men who were left, crawled away to their horses and rode home to Foss, and got into the hall; and there sat the goodman, with his wife on one side and his daughter on the other: then they tell out the tidings: that Hakon is fallen and the brethren, and seven other men besides, and the sons of Thorgrim withal.

When Ketilrid heard that, she fell fainting, and when she came to herself, her mother laid heavy words on her. "Now," quoth she, "is thy light-o'-love well seen, and the desire thou hadst toward Viglund:—good it is that ye must needs be parted now."

Then said the goodman: "Why must thou needs turn this blame on her? She loved her brethren so well, that she may well be astonied at hearing of their fall."

"Maybe that it is so," said Thorbiorg; "yet surely I think not. But now the business in hand is to gather a company of men and go slay Thorgrim the Proud, as swiftly as may be."

"Yea, is that our due business?" said Holmkel. "Meseems he at least is sackless of the slaying of those brethren; and as for his sons, they can lose no more than their lives; and soothly, it was but their due to defend themselves."

CHAPTER XVI

KETIL'S SONS COME OUT TO ICELAND

NOW Viglund and Trusty lay among the slain, till Viglund came to himself, and sought after his brother, and found there was yet life in him; wherefore he was minded to do what he might for him there, for he looked not to be of might to bear him to a dwelling: but now he heard the sound of ice breaking on the way, and lo, their father coming with a sledge. So Thorgrim brought Trusty into the sledge and drave him home to Ingialdsknoll; but Viglund rode unholpen. So he set them into an earth-dug house under his bed, and there Olof awaited them, and bound their wounds: there they abode privily, and were fully healed in the end, though they lay full a twelvemonth wounded.

Holmkel let set his sons in mound, and those men who had fallen with them, and that place is now called Mound-knowes.

These things were now told of far and wide, and all thought it great tidings, deeming it well-nigh sooth that Thorgrim's sons were slain.

Thorgrim and Holmkel met, nor did this

matter depart their friendship, and they made peace on such terms that the case should not be brought to law or judgment.   But when Thorbiorg wist thereof, she sent privily to her father Einar, and bade him take up the feud after her sons; and follow up the sons of Thorgrim for full penalty, if yet they lived: and albeit Einar were old, yet he threw himself into this case, and beguilted the sons of Thorgrim to the full at the Thorsness-thing.

And all this came home to the ears of the country-side.

Now Hakon's shipmates sailed away in the summer when they were ready, and made Norway, and coming to Ketil told him throughout how all things had gone: wherefore it seemed to him that the revenge on Thorgrim and his sons was like to be tardy.   Gunnlaug and Sigurd, the sons of Ketil, were come from a viking cruise in those days, and were grown most famous men: Gunnlaug the Masterful had sworn this oath, never to deny to any man a berth in his ship, if so be his life lay thereon; and Sigurd the Sage had sworn never to reward good with evil.

So Ketil told his sons of the fall of Hakon, and bade them fare to Iceland and revenge his shame, and slay Thorgrim the Proud.

They came into this tardily, yet for the prayer's sake of their father they went; but as soon as they came into the main sea there drave a storm down on them, and a mighty wind, and they weltered about right up to winter-nights.   They came on Snowfellness amidst a great fog, and struck on Onverdaness, and were wrecked; so all men got a-land alive, but of the goods was little saved.

Now Thorgrim heard hereof, and who the men were, and rode to meet them, and they took that joyfully, and abode there the winter through.

And now Sigurd began to think much of Helga, though he said but little to her.

And they knew nought of Thorgrim's sons.

But on a time got Gunnlaug a-talking with Sigurd his brother, and said, " Were it not meet that we should seek revenge on Thorgrim, for certes we may have a right good chance against him ? "

Sigurd answered : " It had been better unspoken ; for thus meseems should I reward good with evil, if I were to slay the man who has taken me from shipwreck ; and in every wise doth better and better to me : nay, rather would I defend him than do him a mischief if it should come to such a pass."

So they made an end of talking, and Gunnlaug never got on this talk again with Sigurd. So the winter wears, and those brethren let array their ship, being desirous to be ready to depart against summer-tide.

And some men would be saying that things went sweetly between Helga and Sigurd ; howbeit, it was scarce known openly to all folk.

CHAPTER XVII

THE PARTING OF VIGLUND AND KETILRID

NOW turns the tale to Earl Eric, who became an old man, and died of eld; but Sigmund his son took his possessions after him, but gat no dignity from King Harald, because the King bore all the kin of Thorgrim something of a grudge for his friendship's sake with Ketil.

Helgi had wedded in Norway, but his wife was dead before the tale gets so far as this: he had a daughter called Ragnhild, the fairest of women. So Helgi was weary of Norway, and went to Iceland, and came thither late in the land-settling time, and bought land in Gautwick of that Gaut who had settled the land there; and there he dwelt till old age.

Now tells the tale of more folk: Steinolf, to wit, who dwelt in Hraundale, who had a son hight Thorleif, a big man and a proper. This Thorleif wooed Ketilrid, but she would nought of him. Then Thorleif made many words about it, to the end that he should get her, howsoever she might gainsay it; and Thorbiorg was utterly of his way of thinking.

But now, when Thorgrim's sons were clean healed of their hurts, they asked their father what he would counsel them to do. He said, "I deem it good rede for you to take berth in the ship of the brethren Gunnlaug and Sigurd, and pray a passage of them over the Iceland sea, saying that your lives lie thereon, as the sooth is, keeping your names hidden meanwhile. Then shall Sigurd keep to his oath, and grant you passage: for this Sigurd is a good man and true, and ye will get but good at his hands: and soothly ye will need it, for over there ye will have to answer for me."

So it was settled that this was to be done. Men say that Ketilrid was weighed down with sorrow that winter; that oft she slept little, and sat awake in her sewing-bower night-long. But that same night before the day whenas Viglund should fare to the ship, for now Ketil's sons were all ready for sea, Viglund and Trusty went to Foss, and into the chamber whereas sat Ketilrid awake, while her handmaids slept.

Sweetly she welcomed the brethren. "It is long since we met," said she; "but right good it is that ye are whole and about on your feet again."

So the two brethren sat down beside her, and talked a long while; and Viglund told her all he was minded to do, and she was glad thereat.

"All is right well," she said, "so long as thou art well, howsoever it fare with me."

M

"Let thyself not be wedded whiles I am away," said Viglund.

"My father must rule that," she said, "for I have no might herein; moreover, I will not be against him : but belike it will be no happier for me than for thee, if things go otherwise : yet all must needs go its own ways."

Then Viglund bade her cut his hair and wash his head, and she did so ; and when it was done, Viglund said : "This I swear, that none shall cut my hair or wash my head but thou only while thou art alive."

Then they all went out together, and parted without in the home-mead : and Viglund kissed Ketilrid weeping sore ; and it was well seen of them, that their hearts were sore to part thus : but so must it be : and she went into her bower, but they went on their way.

And Viglund, or ever he parted from Ketilrid, sang this stave :—

> "Maiden, my songs remember,
>   Fair mouth, if thou mayst learn them ;
>   For, clasp-mead, they may gain thee
>   At whiles some times beguiling.
>   Most precious, when thou wendest
>   Abroad, where folk are gathered,
>   Me, O thou slender isle-may,
>   Each time shalt thou remember."

But when they were come a little way from the garth Viglund sang another stave :—

> "Amid the town we twain stood,
>   And there she wound around me

> Her hands, the hawk-eyed woman,
> The fair-haired, greeting sorely.
> Fast fell tears from the maiden,
> And sorrow told of longing;
> Her cloth the drift-white dear one
> Over bright brows was drawing."

A little after, when Ketilrid came into her bower, thither came the goodman Holmkel, and saw his daughter weeping sorely: then he asked her why she was so sleepless: but for all answer she sang:—

> "A little way I led him,
> The lord of sheen, from green garth;
> But farther than all faring,
> My heart it followeth after.
> Yea, longer had I led him,
> If land lay off the haven,
> And all the waste of Ægir
> Were into green meads waxen."

Then spake Ketilrid and answered her father: "My brothers' death was in my mind."

"Wilt thou have them avenged?" said he.

"That should be soon seen," she said, "if I were as much a man and of might in matters, as I am now but a woman."

The goodman said: "Daughter, know in good sooth, that it is for thy sake that I have done nought against those brethren; for I wot well that they are alive: so come now, hide not from me how thou wouldst have the matter go; for I will get them slain if that is thy will."

"So far from having them slain," said she, "if I might rule, I would never have made them outlaws if I might have ruled ; and, moreover, I would have given them money for their journey if I had had it ; and never would I have any other but Viglund, if I might choose."

Then Holmkel arose and went forth, and took his horse and rode after the brethren. But when they saw him, then said Trusty, "There rideth Holmkel alone ; and if thou wilt get Ketilrid, there is one thing to be done—nought good though it be—to slay Holmkel and carry off Ketilrid."

Said Viglund : "Though it were on the board that I should never see Ketilrid from this time henceforward, yet rather would I have it so than that I do Holmkel any hurt, and forget the trustiness he hath dealt me withal, when he hath had such sorrow to pay me back for : yea, moreover, Ketilrid hath grief enow to bear though she see not her father slain, who hath ever wished all things good for her."

" Yea, so it is best," said Trusty.

" Now shall we," said Viglund, " ride into our home-mead to meet him, for the increasing of his honour."

They did so ; but Holmkel rode on past them and then turned back : so the brethren went back to the road, and found money there, and a gold ring, and a rune-staff : and on the rune-staff were cut all those words of Ketilrid and Holmkel, and this withal, that she gave that money to Viglund.

CHAPTER XVIII

THE SONS OF THORGRIM FARE OUT FROM ICELAND

THEREAFTER they went to the ship, and Gunnlaug and his brother were ready for sea, and the wind blowing off shore : so Viglund hailed the ship, and asked whether Gunnlaug were aboard, and whether he would give them passage over the Iceland seas. He asked who they were : they said one was named Troubleman, and the other Hardfellow. Then Gunnlaug asked what dragged them toward the outlands; and they said, very fear for their lives. So he bade them come out to the ship, and they did so. Then they hoisted sail, and sailed out to sea ; and when they had made some way Gunnlaug said, " Big fellow, why art thou named Troubleman ? "

" Well," said he, " I am called Troubleman, because I have troubles enough and to spare of my own; but I am also called Viglund, and my brother here is Trusty, and we are the sons of Thorgrim the Proud."

Then Gunnlaug was silent, but spake at last :

"What do we, brother Sigurd?" said he; "for now have we a hard matter to get out of, seeing that I wot well that Ketil our father will let slay them as soon as they come to Norway."

Said Sigurd: "Thou didst not ask me this when thou tookest them in; but I knew Viglund when I saw him, by Helga his sister. But meseems thou hast might to bring it about that our father Ketil have no more power over them than thou wilt; and a most meet reward will that be for that wherein Thorgrim has done well to us."

"It is well spoken," said Gunnlaug: "let us do so."

Now they had a fair wind and made Norway, and fared home to Raumsdale, and Ketil was from home; and when he came home, there were his sons in the hall, with Thorgrim's sons sitting in their midst; and they were a company of four-and-twenty.

Now they greeted not their father when he set him down in the high seat; but he knew his sons, but not the sons of Thorgrim: so he asked why they greeted him not, or who the stranger men were.

And Sigurd said, "One is called Viglund, and the other Trusty, the sons of Thorgrim the Proud."

Said Ketil: "Stand up, all ye my men, and take them! And I would that Thorgrim the Proud also were come hither; and then should they all fare by one road."

Sigurd the Sage answered and said: "Great is

the difference between us here and Thorgrim the Proud; for he took us brethren from shipwreck, and did to us ever better and better, when he had us utterly at his will : but thou wilt slay his sons sackless : and belike, good fellows, we may do you a mischief before Thorgrim's sons be slain : and one fate shall be over us all."

Then Ketil says that it is unmeet for him to fight against his own sons, and the wrath runs off him.

Then spake Sigurd : "This is my counsel, that my brother Gunnlaug take the whole matter in hand, for he is well proven in rightfulness."

"Well, it must be so," said Ketil, "rather than that we, father and sons, begin an ill strife together."

So this was settled to be ; and Gunnlaug spake : "This is my doom : Thorgrim shall keep the woman himself; but withal she shall forego the heritage of Earl Thorir her father, and my father shall duly take the said heritage; and my father shall give his daughter Ingibiorg to Trusty, Thorgrim's son; and Sigurd the Sage shall wed Helga, Thorgrim's daughter. And this my doom I hold to firmly."

All thought it done well and wisely, and Ketil was well pleased with matters having come hereto.

So there they abode in good entertainment, the winter through, and Trusty wedded Ingibiorg : but in the summer they went a-warring, all the foster-brethren together, and became the most renowned of men, but Viglund bare away the prize from them all: and they were close upon three winters in this warfare.

But Viglund was never in more joyous mood than at the first; for Ketilrid was never out of his mind.

CHAPTER XIX

THE WEDDING OF KETILRID

NOW must the story be taken up, whereas goodman Holmkel sat at home at Foss. And on a day he rode to Ingialdsknoll, and no man knew what he spake to Thorgrim: and thereafter he went home. Still Thorleif Steinolfson was importunate in the wooing of Ketilrid; but she was slow enough over it.

A little after Thorgrim sent three of his men from home, and they were away three weeks, and when they came home none knew what their errand had been.

Now this befell one day at Foss, that thither came thirty men. Holmkel asked their leader to name himself; and he said he was called Thord, and had his abode in the Eastfirths, and that his errand thither was the wooing of Ketilrid. The goodman put the matter before his daughter, and she was asked thereof, and she said it was as far as might be from her mind, for she deemed the man old, and she said she had no heart to be wedded at all.

Thorbiorg was exceeding eager that the bar-

gain should be struck, and the end of it was,
that Holmkel betrothed her to Thord, whether
she were lieve or loth; and she went away with
Thord at once, and the wedding was to be in
the Eastfirths. So they made no stay till they
got home, and Ketilrid took the rule of all
things there; yet men never saw her glad.

But Thord wedded her not; they both lay in
one bed, but in such wise that there was a curtain
between them.

So wore away a long space.

Thorleif was ill content that Ketilrid was
wedded; but thought it not easy to do aught,
whereas she was a long way off.

Thord did well to Ketilrid in all wise, but
no gain that seemed to Ketilrid, because of the
love she had for Viglund: for ever she bare
about the flame of desire in her breast for his
sake.

CHAPTER XX

VIGLUND COMES OUT TO ICELAND AGAIN

VIGLUND and all the foster-brethren came home that summer from warfare, and Ketil gave them good welcome.

On a day were folk called to head-washing, but Viglund answered thereto: "Nay, I will have nought of this head-washing, nor have I since we parted, Ketilrid and I." Then he sang a stave:—

> "The linen-oak bath-lovely
> Laid last on me the lather:
> So nought have I to hurry
> Unto another head-bath.
> And me no more shall any
> Gold glittering of the maidens
> Henceforth, in all my life-days,
> In ashen bath bewash me."

Nor would Viglund let himself be bathed.

So there they abode in peace that winter; but in summer they made ready for Iceland, each company in their own ship; so they sailed into the sea, and parted company at sea; and Ketil's sons made White-water, and went to quarters at Ingialdsknoll, and told Thorgrim of the peace made twixt him and Ketil, and also that his sons were soon to be looked for : and Thorgrim was glad at all these things. But Viglund and his brother sailed on till they saw Snowfell-Jokul ; then sang Viglund a stave :—

> " Behold the hill whereunder
> My bond of love high-hearted,
> My well-beloved one sitteth :
> Lo Love's eyes turn I to her.
> Sweet, sing I of the gold-brent,
> The proud by proud that sitteth.
> O hill-side among hill-sides,
> Beloved, if any have been ! "

And again he sang :—

> " Leek-bearer, bright the looking
> Over the heaths sun-litten,
> The sun sinks slow thereunder :
> How sore I long to be there !
> Lovesome she makes the mountains ;
> Sweet, therefore must I hush me :
> The goodliest goddess have I
> To greet, who sits thereunder."

And therewith there came a wind down from the ness so great, that they drave out into the sea ; and a west wind fell on them, and the weather became exceeding stormy, and men must ever stand a-baling. And on a day, as Viglund sat on the bulk amid weather of the roughest, he sang :—

> " Ketilrid her carle bade
> Quail not mid swift sailing,
> Though the beat of billows
> Overbore the foredeck.

Still her word is with me,
Be we wight now, Trusty!
Stormy heart of sorrow
I have for Ketilrid."

"A mighty matter, forsooth," said Trusty, "whenas thou must needs name her first and last in thy singing."

"Yea, kinsman, thinkest thou so?" said Viglund.

So they were out at sea many days, and at last amid great danger and pain made Gautwick in the Eastfirths.

Then said Viglund, "Whereas we have a feud on us, methinks it were well, brother, that thou shouldst call thyself Raven, and I should call myself Erne."

So the goodman from the stead of Gautwick came to the ship; and the shipmen gave him good welcome, and bade him take what he would of the lading. The goodman said he had a young wife. "She," quoth he, "shall come to the ship and take of your lading what she will." So the goodman rode home now, and the mistress came thither the next morning; and she knew Viglund as soon as she saw him, but made little of it; but Viglund was much astonied when he knew her.

So she took what she would of the lading, for all things were at her will.

The bonder had bidden the ship-masters home, and when they came thither, the master and mistress went to meet them: then stumbled the goodman, for he was stiff with eld: then the mistress said, somewhat under her breath, "An evil mate is an old man."

"It was so slippery, though," said the master.

So they were brought in with all honour; but Viglund deemed that Ketilrid knew him not. But she sang :—

> "The fight-grove of Van's fire,
> The fair, I knew at even—
> Marvel that he would meet me!
> I knew gold-master Trusty.
> The ship of gold all slender
> To such an one is wedded,
> That ne'er another older
> In all the world one findeth."

So they abode there that winter, and Viglund was exceeding heavy-hearted, but Trusty as blithe as might be, and the goodman exceeding blithe, who served them with all kindness.

But it is told that Ketilrid had a veil ever before her face, for she would not that Viglund should know her, and that Viglund also for his part was not all so sure that it was she.

CHAPTER XXI

GUESTING AT GAUTWICK

ON a day Ketilrid was standing without, and she was exceeding warm, and had rent the veil from her face : and in that nick of time Viglund came out and saw her visage clearly ; and thereat was he much astonied, and flushed red as blood. He went into the hall, wherein was Trusty sitting, who asked him what was toward and what he had seen that he was so changed. Then Viglund sang a stave :—

> "Nought shall I say thee lie now :
> Ne'er saw I eyen sweeter
> Since when we twain were sundered,
> O sweet one of the worm-lair.
> This craven carle her clippeth ;
> Shall I not carve from off him
> His head ? all grief go with him !—
> Grief from the gold one gat I."

Now Ketilrid never had a veil before her face from that time forward that she wotted that Viglund knew her.

So Trusty said, "The last thing to be done I deem is to do the goodman any harm, as well as he has done to us; a luckless deed it will be to slay her husband sackless: let it be far from thee!" And he sang :—

> "Never, burnt-rings breaker,
>   Shall ye be brought together.
> If felon's deed thou doest
>   On Fafnir's-land's good dealer.
> Not ever, nor in all things,
>   Availeth shielded onset;
> Aright must we arede us,
>   O brother wise in trials."

So the day wears away to evening, and folk go to rest. But in the night Viglund arose and went to the bed wherein slept Ketilrid and the goodman; the light was drawn up into the hall roof, so that aloft it was light, but all below was dim. So he lifted up the curtains and saw Ketilrid lying turned towards the wall, and the goodman turned away thence towards the bed-stock, with his head laid thereon, handy to be smitten off.

Then was Viglund at the point to draw his sword, but therewith came Trusty to him, and said, "Nay, beware of thyself, and do no such fearful and shameful deed as to slay a sleeping man. Let none see in thee that thy heart is in this woman! bear thyself like a man!" And he sang :—

> "My friend, mind here the maiden
>   Who murdereth all thy gladness;
> See there thy fair fame's furtherer,
>   Who seemeth fain of saying:

> Though one, the lovely woman,
> Hath wasted all thy life-joy,
> Yet keep it close within thee, -
> Nor cry aloud thereover."

Therewith was Viglund appeased, and he wondered withal that there was so wide a space in the bed betwixt them.

So the brethren went to their beds; but Viglund slept but little that night, and the next morning was he exceeding downcast; but the goodman was very joyous, and he asked Viglund what made him so sorrowful.

Then Viglund, whom all deemed was called Erne, sang a stave :—

> "The white hands' ice-hill's wearer
> Hath wasted all my joyance:
> O strong against me straineth
> The stream of heaped-up waters!
> This sapling oak thy wife here
> From out my heart ne'er goeth;
> Well of tormenting wotteth
> The woman mid her playing."

"Like enough it is so," said the master; "but come, it were good that we disported us and played at the chess."

And they did so; but little heed had Erne of the board because of the thought he had of the goodwife, so that he was like to be mated: but therewith came the mistress thither, and looked on the board, and sang this half-stave :—

> "O battles' thunder-bearer
> Be glad and shift thy board-piece
> On to this square thou seest;
> So saith the staff of hangings."

N

Then the master looked on her and sang :—

> " Again to-day gold-goddess
> Against her husband turneth,
> Though I the wealth-god owe thee
> For nought but eld meseemeth."

So Erne played as he was bidden, and the game
was a drawn game.

The goodwife talked little with Erne; but
on a day when they met without alone, they two,
Viglund and Ketilrid, they did talk together
somewhat; yet not for long; and when they
had made an end of talking, Viglund sang :—

> "O slender sweet, O fair-browed,
> Meseemeth this thy husband
> As ferry-boat all foredone
> Amid the Skerries floating.
> But thee, when I behold thee
> Go forth so mighty waxen,
> 'Tis as a ship all stately
> O'er sea-mews' pasture sweeping."

Then they left off talking, and Ketilrid went
in; but Erne fell to talk with the goodman,
who was joyous with the shipmaster; but Erne
sang :—

> " Friend, watch and ward now hold thou
> Of this thy wife, the fair one;
> And heed lest that spear-Goddess
> Should go about to waste me.
> If oft we meet without doors,
> I and the twined-thread's Goddess,
> Who knows whose most she should be,
> Or mine or thine, that gold-wife?"

And another stave he sang :—

> "Fight-grove full fain would not
> Be found amidst of man-folk,
> So tame to maids' enticing
> To take a man's wife wedded.
> But if amid the mirk-tide
> She came here made as woman,
> I cannot soothly swear it
> But soft I should enfold her."

Said the master; "O, all will go well enough
if she sees to it herself." And so they left this
talk.

Ever did the goodman do better and better to
the shipmaster, but it availed him nought; a
sorrowful man he was ever, and never spake one
joyous word. But Trusty, his brother, thought
such harm of this, that he talked to him full oft,
bidding him put it from his mind and take another woman. But Erne said, "It may not be;
I should not love her; yea, moreover, I could
not set the thing afoot." And he sang :—

> "Another man's wife love I,
> Unmanly am I holden,
> Though old, and on her beam-ends,
> Fallen is the fallow oak-keel.
> I wot not if another,
> At any time hereafter,
> Shall be as sweet unto me—
> The ship drave out of peril."

"It may be so," said Raven. So they went
together into the hall: and there sat the master
with the goodwife on his knees, and he with his

arms about her middle : but Erne saw that she was not right glad thereat.

Now she slipped from his knees, and went and sat down on the bench, and wept. Erne went thither, and sat down by her, and they talked together softly. And he sang :—

> " Sweet linen-bride, full seldom
> In such wise would I find thee,
> An hoary dotard's hand-claws
> Hanging about thee, bright one.
> Rather, O wristfires' lady,
> Would I around thy midmost
> Cast as my longing led me,
> These lands of gold light-shining."

" Mayhappen," said the goodwife, " it will never be." Therewith she arose and went away : but the master was exceeding joyous and said : " Now, Erne, I will that thou have care of my household, and all else that concerns me, whiles I am away, because I am going from home and shall be away for a month at the least ; and thee I trust best of all in all matters that concern me."

Erne said little to this.

CHAPTER XXII

A WEDDING AT GAUTWICK

THEN the master went from home with fourteen men; and when he was gone Erne spake to his brother and said: "Methinks it were well if we went from home, and abode not here whiles the master is away; for otherwise folk will deem that I am about beguiling his wife; and then would a mighty difference be seen betwixt me and the master."

So they rode from home, and abode by their shipmates till the goodman came home on the day named.

And now were there many more with him than before: for in his company were Thorgrim the Proud, and Olof his wife, and Helga his daughter, and Sigurd the Sage, and Gunnlaug his brother, and Holmkel the master of Foss: and they were fifty all told. Therewith also came home the two mariners.

And now Ketilrid had arrayed all things as the goodman had commanded her, with the intent to hold his wedding.

But when they were all set down in the hall
the master stood up and said : " So stands the
case, Shipmaster Erne, that thou hast abided here
through the winter, and thy brother with thee,
and I know that thou art called Viglund and thy
brother Trusty, and that ye are the sons of
Thorgrim the Proud : no less I know all thy
mind toward Ketilrid ; and with many trials and
troubles have I tried thee, and all hast thou borne
well : nevertheless thy brother hath holpen thee
that thou hast not fallen into any dreadful case
or done any dreadful thing : and I myself indeed
had ever something else to fall back upon.   For
now will I no longer hide from thee that I am
called Helgi, and am the son of Earl Eric, and
thine own father's brother : therefore wooed I
Ketilrid, that I might keep her safe for thee, and
she is a clean maiden as for me.   Ketilrid hath
borne all well and womanly : for I and the others
hid these things from her : forsooth we have lain
never under one sheet, for the bedstock cometh up
between the berths we lay in, though we had one
coverlet over all : and I deem indeed that it
would be no trial nor penance to her though she
knew no man whiles thou wert alive.   But all
these things were done by the rede of Master
Holmkel, and methinks it were well that thou
pray him for peace, and crave his daughter of him
thereafter : and surely he will give thee peace,
for things better and nobler than this he hath
done to thee in your dealings together."

Then went Viglund to Master Holmkel, and laid his head on his knee, and bade him do therewith whatso he would; and he answered in this wise—

"That shall be done with thine head which shall please my daughter Ketilrid best, and assuredly we will be at peace together."

So Holmkel gave his daughter Ketilrid to Viglund, and Thorgrim gave Helga his daughter to Sigurd the Sage, and Helgi gave Ragnhild his daughter to Gunnlaug the Masterful; and folk sat down to all these weddings at one and the same time.

Then each went to his own house: Viglund and Ketilrid loved their life exceeding well now, and dwelt at Foss after Holmkel, Ketilrid's father: but Gunnlaug the Masterful and Sigurd his brother fared abroad and set up house in Norway: but Trusty abode at Ingialdsknoll after Thorgrim his father.

SO HERE ENDETH THE TALE

"Whoso thinketh this good game,
God keep us all from hurt and grame;
And may all things have such an end
That all we unto God may wend.
He who to tell this tale hath will,
He needeth no long time be still;
For here we cast off pain and woe,
Here noble deeds may Champions know,
Manners and tales and glorious lore,
And truth withal that shall endure,

Thanks to him who hearkened it,
Yea and unto him who writ,
And Thorgeir that engrossed it fair.
God's and Mary's grace be here!"

Two sons and a father did write this book: pray ye to God for them all.   Amen.

THE TALE OF
HOGNI AND HEDINN

THE TALE OF

HOGNI AND HEDINN

CHAPTER I

OF FREYIA AND THE DWARFS

EAST of Vanaquisl in Asia was the land called Asialand or Asiahome, but the folk that dwelt there was called Æsir, and their chief town was Asgard. Odin was the name of the king thereof, and therein was a right holy place of sacrifice. Niord and Frey Odin made Temple-priests thereover; but the daughter of Niord was Freyia, and she was fellow to Odin and his concubine.

Now there were certain men in Asia, whereof one was called Alfrigg, the second Dwalin, the third Berling, the fourth Grerr: these had their abode but a little space from the King's hall, and were men so wise in craftsmanship, that they laid skilful hand on all matters; and such-like men as they were did men call dwarfs. In a rock was their dwelling, and in that day they mingled more with menfolk than as now they do.

Odin loved Freyia full sore, and withal she was the fairest woman of that day : she had a bower that was both fair and strong ; insomuch, say men, that if the door were shut to, none might come into the bower aforesaid without the will of Freyia.

Now on a day went Freyia afoot by that rock of the dwarfs, and it lay open : therein were the dwarfs a-smithying a golden collar, and the work was at point to be done : fair seemed that collar to Freyia, and fair seemed Freyia to the dwarfs.

Now would Freyia buy the collar of them, and bade them in return for it silver and gold, and other good things. They said they lacked not money, yet that each of them would sell his share of the collar for this thing, and for nought else— that she should lie a night by each of them : wherefore, whether she liked it better or worse, on such wise did she strike the bargain with them ; and so the four nights being outworn, and all conditions fulfilled, they delivered the collar to Freyia ; and she went home to her bower, and held her peace hereof, as if nought had befallen.

CHAPTER II

OF THE STEALING OF FREYIA'S COLLAR, AND
HOW SHE MAY HAVE IT AGAIN

THERE was a man called Farbauti, which
carl had to wife a carline called Laufey;
she was both slim and slender, therefore was she
called Needle.   One child had these, a son called
Loki; nought great of growth was he, but betimes shameless of tongue and nimble in gait;
over all men had he that craft which is called
cunning; guileful was he from his youth up,
therefore was he called Loki the Sly.

He betook himself to Odin at Asgard and
became his man.   Ever had Odin a good word
for him, whatsoever he turned to; yet withal he
oft laid heavy labours upon him, which forsooth
he turned out of hand better than any man looked
for : moreover, he knew wellnigh all things that
befell, and told all he knew to Odin.

So tells the tale that Loki knew how that
Freyia had gotten the collar, yea and what she
had given for it; so he told Odin thereof, and
when Odin heard of it he bade Loki get the
collar and bring it to him.   Loki said it was not

a likely business, because no man might come into Freyia's bower without the will of her ; but Odin bade him go his ways and not come back before he had gotten the collar. Then Loki turned away howling, and most of men were glad thereof whenas Loki throve nought.

But Loki went to Freyia's bower, and it was locked ; he strove to come in, and might not ; and cold it was without, so that he fast began to grow a-cold.

So he turned himself into a fly, and fluttered about all the locks and the joints, and found no hole therein whereby he might come in, till up by the gable-top he found a hole, yet no bigger than one might thrust a needle through ; none the less he wriggled in thereby. So when he was come in he peered all about to see if any waked, but soon he got to see that all were asleep in the bower. Then in he goeth unto Freyia's bed, and sees that she hath the collar on her with the clasp turned downward. Thereon Loki changed himself into a flea, and sat on Freyia's cheek, and stung her so that she woke and turned about, and then fell asleep again. Then Loki drew from off him his flea's shape, and undid the collar, and opened the bower, and gat him gone to Odin therewith.

Next morn awoke Freyia and saw that the doors were open, yet unbroken, and that the goodly collar was gone. She deemed she knew what guile had wrought it, so she goeth into the hall when she is clad, and cometh before Odin the

king, and speaketh to him of the evil he has let
be wrought against her in the stealing of that dear
thing, and biddeth him give her back her jewel.

Odin says that in such wise hath she gotten it,
that never again shall she have it. " Unless forsooth thou bring to pass, that two kings, each
served of twenty kings, fall to strife, and fight
under such weird and spell, that they no sooner
fall adown than they stand up again and fight on :
always unless some christened man be so bold of
heart, and the fate and fortune of his lord be so
great, that he shall dare go into that battle, and
smite with weapons these men : and so first shall
their toil come to an end, to whatsoever lord it
shall befall to loose them from the pine and
trouble of their fell deeds."

Hereto said Freyia yea, and gat her collar
again.

CHAPTER III

OF KING ERLING, AND SORLI HIS SON

IN those days, when four-and-twenty winters were worn away from the death of Peace-Frodi, a king ruled over the Uplands in Norway called Erling. He had a queen and two sons; Sorli the Strong the elder, and Erlend the younger : hopeful were they both, but Sorli was the stronger. They fell to warfare so soon as they were of age thereto ; they fought with the viking Sindri, son of Sveigr, the son of Haki, the sea-king, at the Elfskerries ; and there fell the viking Sindri and all his folk ; there also fell Erlend Erlingson. Thereafter Sorli sailed into the East-salt-sea, and harried there, and did so many doughty deeds that late it were ere all were written down.

CHAPTER IV

SORLI SLAYETH KING HALFDAN

THERE was a king hight Halfdan, who ruled over Denmark, and abode in a stead called Roi's-well; he had to wife Hvedna the old, and their sons were Hogni and Hakon, men peerless of growth and might, and all prowess : they betook them to warfare so soon as they were come to man's estate.

Now cometh the tale on Sorli again, for on an autumn-tide he sailed to Denmark. King Halfdan was minded as at this time to go to an assembly of the kings ; he was well stricken in years when these things betid. He had a dragon so good that never was such another ship in all Norway for strength's sake, and all craftsmanship. Now was this ship lying moored in the haven, but King Halfdan was a-land and had let brew his farewell drink. But when Sorli saw the dragon, so great covetise ran into his heart that he must needs have her : and forsooth, as most men say, no ship so goodly hath been in the Northlands, but it were the dragon Ellida, or Gnod, or the Long Worm.

o

So Sorli spake to his men, bidding them array them for battle; "for we will slay King Halfdan and have away his dragon."

Then answered his word a man called Sævar, his Forecastle-man and Marshal: "Ill rede, lord," saith he; "for King Halfdan is a mighty lord of great renown, and hath two sons to avenge him, who are either of them full famous men."

"Let them be mightier than the very Gods," said Sorli, "yet shall I none the less join battle."

So they arrayed them for the fight.

Now came tidings hereof to King Halfdan, and he started up and fared down to the ships with his men, and they got them ready for battle.

Some men set before King Halfdan that it was ill rede to fight, and it were best to flee away because of the odds; but the king said that they should fall every one across the other's feet or ever he should flee. So either side arrayed them, and joined battle of the fiercest; the end whereof was such that King Halfdan fell and all his folk, and Sorli took his dragon and all that was of worth.

Thereafter heard Sorli that Hogni was come from warfare, and lay by Odins-isle; so thitherward straight stood Sorli, and when they met he told him of the fall of Halfdan his father, and offered him atonement and self-doom, and they to become foster-brethren. But Hogni gainsayed him utterly: so they fought as it

sayeth in Sorli's Song. Hakon went forth full
fairly, and slew Sævar, Sorli's Banner-bearer and
Forecastle-man, and therewith Sorli slew Hakon,
and Hogni slew Erling the king, Sorli's father.

Then they fought together, Hogni and Sorli,
and Sorli fell before Hogni for wounds and
weariness' sake: but Hogni let heal him, and
they swore the oath of brotherhood thereafter,
and held it well whiles they both lived. Sorli
was the shortest-lived of them; he fell in the
East-sea before the vikings, as it saith in the
Sorli-Song, and here saith:—

> " Fell there the fight-greedy,
> Foremost of war-host,
> Eager in East-seas,
> All on Hells' hall-floor;
> Died there the doughty
> In dale-fishes joy-tide,
> With byrny-rod biting
> The vikings in brand-thing."

But when Hogni heard of the fall of Sorli, he
went a warring in the Eastlands that same summer,
and had the victory in every place, and became
king thereover; and so say men that twenty kings
paid tribute to King Hogni, and held their realms
of him.

Hogni won so great fame from his doughty
deeds and his warfare that he was as well known
by name north in the Finn-steads, as right away
in Paris-town; yea, and all betwixt and between.

CHAPTER V

HEDINN HEARETH TELL OF KING HOGNI, AND COMETH TO THE NORTHLANDS

HIARANDI was the name of a king who ruled over Serkland; a queen he had, and one son named Hedinn, who from his youth up was peerless of growth, and strength, and prowess: from his early days he betook him to warfare, and became a Sea-king, and harried wide about Spain and the land of the Greeks, and all realms thereabout, till twenty kings paid tribute to him, and held of him land and fief.

On a winter abode Hedinn at home in Serkland, and it is said that on a time he went into the wood with his household; and so it befell him to be alone of his men in a certain wood-lawn, and there in the wood-lawn he saw a woman sitting on a chair, great of growth and goodly of aspect: he asked her of her name, and she named herself Gondul.

Then fell they a-talking, and she asked him of his doughty deeds, and lightly he told her all, and asked her if she wotted of any king who was his peer in daring and hardihood, in fame and further-

ance; and she said she wotted of one who fell
nowise short of him, and who was served of
twenty kings no less than he, and that his name
was Hogni, and his dwelling north in Denmark.

"Then wot I," said Hedinn, "that we shall
try it which of us twain is foremost."

"Now will it be time for thee to go to thy
men," said Gondul; "they will be seeking thee."

So they departed and he fared to his men, but
she was left sitting there.

But so soon as spring was come Hedinn arrayed
his departure, and had a dragon and three hundred
men thereon : he made for the Northlands, and
sailed all that summer and winter, and came to
Denmark in the Springtide.

CHAPTER VI

HOGNI AND HEDINN MEET, AND SWEAR
BROTHERHOOD TO EACH OTHER

KING Hogni sat at home this while, and when he heard tell how a noble king is come to his land he bade him home to a glorious feast, and that Hedinn took. And as they sat at the drink, Hogni asked what errand Hedinn had thither, that had driven him so far north in the world. Hedinn said that this was his errand, that they twain should try their hardihood and daring, their prowess and all their craftsmanship; and Hogni said he was all ready thereto.

So betimes on the morrow fared they to swimming and shooting at marks, and strove in tilting and fencing and all prowess; and in all skill were they so alike that none thought he could see betwixt them which was the foremost. Thereafter they swore themselves foster-brethren, and should halve all things between them.

Hedinn was young and unwedded, but Hogni was somewhat older, and he had to wife Hervor, daughter of Hiorvard, who was the son of Heidrek, who was the son of Wolfskin.

Hogni had a daughter, Hild by name, the fairest and wisest of all women, and he loved his daughter much.   No other child had he.

CHAPTER VII

THE BEGUILING OF HEDINN, AND OF HIS EVIL DEED

THE tale telleth that Hogni went a-warring a little hereafter, and left Hedinn behind to ward the realm. So on a day went Hedinn into the wood for his disport, and blithe was the weather. And yet again he turned away from his men and came into a certain wood-lawn, and there in the lawn beheld the same woman sitting in a chair, whom he had seen aforetime in Serkland, and him seemed that she was now gotten fairer than aforetime.

Yet again she first cast a word at him, and became kind in speech to him; she held a horn in her hand shut in with a lid, and the king's heart yearned toward her.

She bade the king drink, and he was thirsty, for he was gotten warm; so he took the horn and drank, and when he had drunk, lo a marvellous change came over him, for he remembered nought of all that was betid to him aforetime, and he sat him down and talked with her. She asked whether he had tried, as she had bidden him, the prowess of Hogni and his hardihood.

Hedinn said that sooth it was : " For he fell short of me in nought in any mastery we tried : so now are we called equal."

" Yet are ye nought equal," said she.

" Whereby makest thou that ? " said he.

" In this wise," said she ; " that Hogni hath a queen of high kindred, but thou hast no wife."

He answers : " Hogni will give me Hild, his daughter, so soon as I ask her ; and then am I no worse wedded than he."

" Minished were thy glory then," she said, " wert thou to crave Hogni of alliance. Better were it, if forsooth thou lack neither hardihood nor daring according to thy boast, that thou have away Hild, and slay the Queen in this wise : to wit, to lay her down before the beak of that dragon-ship, and let smite her asunder therewith in the launching of it."

Now so was Hedinn ensnared by evil heart and forgetfulness, because of the drink he had drunken, that nought seemed good to him save this ; and he clean forgat that he and Hogni were foster-brethren.

So they departed, and Hedinn fared to his men ; and this befell when summer was far spent.

Now Hedinn ordained his men for the arraying of the dragon, saying that he would away for Serkland. Then went he to the bower, and took Hild and the queen, one by either hand, and went forth with them ; and his men took Hild's raiment and fair things. Those men only were in the realm, who durst do nought for Hedinn and his men; for full fearful of countenance was he.

But Hild asked Hedinn what he would, and he told her; and she bade him do it not: "For," quoth she, "my father will give me to thee if thou woo me of him."

"I will not do so much as to woo thee," said Hedinn.

"And though," said she, "thou wilt do no otherwise than bear me away, yet may my father be appeased thereof: but if thou do this evil deed and unmanly, doing my mother to death, then never may my father be appeased: and this wise have my dreams pointed, that ye shall fight and lay each other a-low; and then shall yet heavier things fall upon you: and great sorrow shall it be to me, if such a fate must fall upon my father that he must bear a dreadful weird and heavy spells: nor have I any joy to see thee sore-hearted under bitter toil."

Hedinn said he heeded nought what should come after, and that he would do his deed none the less.

"Yea, thou mayest none other do," said Hild, "for not of thyself dost thou it."

Then went Hedinn down to the strand, and the dragon was thrust forth, and the queen laid down before the beak thereof; and there she lost her life.

So went Hedinn aboard the dragon: but when all was dight he would fain go a-land alone of his men, and into the self-same wood wherein he had

gone aforetime: and so, when he was come into
the wood-lawn, there saw he Gondul sitting in a
chair: they greeted each the other friendly, and
then Hedinn told her of his deeds, and thereof
was she well content.   She had with her the horn
whereof he had drunk afore, and again she bade
him drink thereof; so he took it and drank, and
when he had drunk sleep came upon him, and he
fell tottering into her lap: but when he slept she
drew away from his head and spake: "Now
hallow I thee, and give thee to lie under all
those spells and the weird that Odin commanded,
thee and Hogni, and all the hosts of you."

Then awoke Hedinn, and saw the ghostly
shadow of Gondul, and him-seemed she was
waxen black and over big; and all things came
to his mind again, and mighty woe he deemed it.
And now was he minded to get him far away
somewhither, lest he hear daily the blame and
shame of his evil deed.

So he went to the ship and they unmoored
speedily: the wind blew off shore, and so he
sailed away with Hild.

CHAPTER VIII

THE WEIRD FALLETH ON THESE TWAIN,
HOGNI AND HEDINN

NOW cometh Hogni home, and comes to wot the sooth, that Hedinn hath sailed away with Hild and the dragon Halfdans-loom, and his queen is left dead there. Full wroth was Hogni thereat, and bade men turn about straightway and sail after Hedinn. Even so did they speedily, and they had a wind of the best, and ever came at eve to the haven whence Hedinn had sailed the morning afore.

But on a day whenas Hogni made the haven, lo the sails of Hedinn in sight on the main; so Hogni, he and his, stood after them; and most sooth is it told that a head-wind fell on Hedinn, whiles the same fair wind went with Hogni.

So Hedinn brought-to at an isle called Ha, and lay in the roadstead there, and speedily came Hogni up with him; and when they met Hedinn greeted him softly: "Needs must I say, foster-brother," saith he, "how evil hath befallen me, that none may amend save thou: for I have taken from thee thy daughter and thy dragon;

and thy queen I have done to death. And yet is this deed done not from my evil heart alone, but rather from wicked witchcraft and evil spells; and now will I that thou alone shear and shape betwixt us. But I will offer thee to forego both Hild and the dragon, my men and all my wealth, and to fare so far out in the world that I may never come into the Northlands again, or thine eye-sight, whiles I live."

Hogni answered: "I would have given thee Hild, hadst thou wooed her; yea, and though thou hadst borne away Hild from me, yet for all that might we have had peace: but whereas thou hast now wrought a dastard's deed in the laying down of my queen and slaying of her, there is no hope that I may ever take atonement from thee; but here, in this place, shall we try straightway which of us twain hath more skill in the smiting of strokes."

Hedinn answered: "Rede it were, since thou wilt nought else but battle, that we twain try it alone, for no man here is guilty against thee saving I alone: and nowise meet it is that guiltless men should pay for my folly and ill-doing."

But the followers of either of them answered as with one mouth, that they would all fall one upon the other rather than that they two should play alone.

So when Hedinn saw that Hogni would nought else but battle, he bade his men go up a-land: "For I will fail Hogni no longer, nor beg off the battle : so let each do according to his manhood."

So they go up a-land now and fight: full fierce is Hogni, and Hedinn apt at arms and mighty of stroke.

Soothly is it said that such mighty and evil spells went with the weird of these, that though they clave each other down to the shoulders, yet still they stood upon their feet and fought on: and ever sat Hild in a grove and looked on the play.

So this travail and torment went on ever from the time they first fell a-fighting till the time that Olaf Tryggvison was king in Norway; and men say that it was an hundred and forty three years before the noble man, King Olaf, brought it so about that his courtman loosed them from this woeful labour and miserable grief of heart.

CHAPTER IX

HOGNI AND HEDINN ARE LOOSED FROM THEIR WEIRD

SO tells the tale, that in the first year of the reign of King Olaf he came to the Isle of Ha, and lay in the haven there on an eve. Now such was the way of things in that isle, that every night whoso watched there vanished away, so that none knew what was become of them.

On this night had Ivar Gleam-bright to hold ward : so when all on ship-board were asleep Ivar took his sword, which Iron-shield of Heathwood had owned erst, and Thorstein his son had given to Ivar, and all his war-gear he took withal, and so went up on to the isle.

But when he was gotten up there, lo a man coming to meet him, great of growth, and all bloody, and exceeding sorrowful of countenance. Ivar asked that man of his name ; and he said he was called Hedinn, the son of Hiarandi, of the blood of Serkland.

"Sooth have I to tell thee," said he, "that whereas the watchmen have vanished away, ye must lay it to me and to Hogni, the son of Halfdan ; for we and our men are fallen under such sore weird and labour, that we fight on both night and day; and so hath it been with us for many generations of men; and Hild, the daughter of Hogni, sitteth by and looketh on. Odin hath laid this weird upon us, nor shall aught loose us therefrom till a christened man fight with us; and then whoso he smiteth down shall rise up no more; and in such wise shall each one of us be loosed from his labour. Now will I crave of thee to go with me to the battle, for I wot that thou art well christened; and thy king also whom thou servest is of great goodhap, of whom my heart telleth me, that of him and his men shall we have somewhat good."

Ivar said yea to going with him; and glad was Hedinn thereat, and said: "Be thou ware not to meet Hogni face to face, and again that thou slay not me before him; for no mortal man may look Hogni in the face, or slay him if I be dead first: for he hath the Ægis-helm in the eyes of him, nor may any shield him thence. So there is but one thing for it, that I face him and fight him, whilst thou goest at his back and so givest him his death-blow; for it will be but easy work for thee to slay me, though I be left alive the longest of us all."

Therewith went they to the battle, and Ivar seeth that all is sooth that Hedinn hath told him: so he goeth to the back of Hogni, and smiteth him into his head, and cleaveth him down to the shoulders: and Hogni fell dead, and never rose up again.

Then slew Ivar all those men who were at the battle, and Hedinn last of all, and that was no hard work for him. But when he came to the grove wherein Hild was wont to sit, lo she was vanished away.

Then went Ivar to the ship, when it was now daybreak, and he came to the king and told him hereof: and the king made much of his deed, and said that it had gone luckily with him.

But the next day they went a-land, and thither where the battle had been, and saw nowhere any signs of what had befallen there: but blood was seen on Ivar's sword as a token thereof; and never after did the watchmen vanish away.

So after these things the king went back to his realm.

THE END OF THIS TALE

THE TALE OF
ROI THE FOOL

THE TALE OF

ROI THE FOOL

CHAPTER I

OF ROI

THERE was a man called Roi who was born and bred in Denmark; he was the son of a good bonder, a man of prowess, and strong enow and of good wit. Roi was ever a-going chaffering, and got money together that wise; a good smith he was to wit, and that way also he got money full oft. In those days King Swein, the son of Harald, who was called Twibeard, ruled over Denmark, and was a king well loved of his folk.

Now on a summer Roi wrecked his ship on the south parts of Denmark, and lost goods and all, though the crew were barely saved. So they went up a-land, and Roi took to smithying, and gat goods thus; he was well loved of his fellows, nor had he long followed this craft before the money grew on his hands, for a full famous smith he was; yet was the story still the same, and he fared but ill with his goods; for as soon as he had gotten together what he would he went to sea and lost it all.

Roi had a mark in the face of him whereby he was lightly known from other men, for one of his eyes was blue and the other black: but a most manly man he was, and ruled his temper well, yea even were he ill dealt with; ever he got wealth a-land, and lost it a-voyaging, and so when he had now thrice lost his ship in his chaffering voyages, he thought he could see, that he was not made for that craft, and yet going from land to land with his merchandise was the thing most to his mind: so he bethought him of going to King Swein, if perchance he might have any counsel of him, for he wotted that he was a man of good counsel, and that many had been the better thereof. Wherefore he went thither, and coming before the king greeted him.

And the king asked, "Who art thou?"

"Roi am I called," said he.

Quoth the king, "Art thou Roi the Come-to-nought?"

He answered, "I am wanting somewhat else from thee than mocks such as these. I would rather of thee the help of thy money and good-hap; maybe it shall avail me, for I would fain hope that thy health and hap may perchance prevail over my ill-luck."

King Swein said: "If thou be minded to seek luck of me it were well, so please you, that we were partners together."

Then said folk to the king, that it were ill-

counselled to be partner of one so unlucky as
Roi, and that he would lose his money at once :
but the king answered—

"It shall be risked which may most prevail, a
king's luck or his ill-luck."

Therewith he gave money to Roi that they
should have together, and Roi went a chaffering
on such covenant with the king, that he should
pay nought if the goods were lost, and share
what there was of gain, and that he should pay the
king as much as he got from him to begin with.
So Roi went his ways, and things went well with
his voyages, and the money grew speedily, and he
came back in autumn-tide to the king with much
wealth ; and no long time was passed before he
became right wealthy, and was now called Roi the
Wealthy, or the Stately, and every summer he
went from land to land, chaffering, on the
covenant aforesaid with the king.

CHAPTER II

OF ROI

NOW on a time spake Roi with the king:
"Now will I that thou take thy share, lord,
lest things go ill and I lose thy goods."

Said the king: "Thou art minded then that
it were better for our partnership to come to an
end: but I was deeming it not ill-counselled for
thee to abide in the land here under my good
keeping, and that thou shouldst wed and dwell
quietly here, with me to further thee. Nor do I
deem it hopeful, this mind of thine for trading;
a slippery matter it seems to me, even as thou
hast proved aforetime." Nevertheless Roi would
have the money shared, and so it was done, and
the king said: "This is thy rede, Roi, and not
mine; and better meseems it had been since thou
hast come to seek luck at my hands that it had
abided by thee." Men took up the word therewith, and said how he himself had proven how
the king's luck had come to him in time of need.
But the king said that Roi had dealt well with
him, and that it would be great scathe if he

tumbled into any ill-luck: and therewithal they parted.

So Roi went on his voyage and had plenteous wealth. He sailed to Sweden this time, and made up the Low, and brought-to off certain meads: and now had Roi all the ship's lading to himself. On a day he went a-land by himself alone, and when he had gone awhile he met a man with red hair and straight, and somewhat of a brisk lad to look on. Roi asked him of his name, and he said he was called Helgi, and was a court-man of King Eric; and he asked withal who the chapman was. Roi told his name, whereon Helgi said he knew him and had seen him before; and therewith he said he would deal with him. Roi asked how much he would deal for, and Helgi answered: "I wot that ye Danes are new come a-land, and I hear say that they are all thy servants, and that all the ship's lading is thine; and I will buy the whole lading of thee if thou wilt."

Roi said he was no whit of a peddler then; and Helgi said he could deal both in small and in great. Then asked Roi: "Where are the goods that I am to take of thee?" Helgi bade him go with him, and said that he would show him that there was no fooling in that his offer. So they went till they came to a storehouse all full of merchandise, and all that was therein Helgi offered Roi for his lading: Roi deemed it good chaffer, and thought that little would be his loss therein though they made a deal of it, and that the wares were good cheap. So it came to this that they struck the bargain, and a flitting-day was appointed between them; wherewith they parted, and Roi went back to his ship.

CHAPTER III

EARL THORGNYR'S TALK WITH HIS
DAUGHTER

THE very next day came Helgi down with many men and beasts, and let flit away the lading, so that all was gone by nightfall; and soothly he had no lack either of men or of yoke-beasts hereto. A few days after Roi went up a-land alone, with the mind to settle matters for the flitting of his wares: and by this time was worn by one night over and above the time that he should have let fetch them. Roi deemed it mattered nought for a night, though he had come later than was appointed; for in sooth he was busied about many things. Roi was clad full goodly, for he was a very showy man, and he had a right noble knife and belt, on either where-of had many a penny been spent: good weapons he had, and a fair scarlet kirtle, with a broidered cloak over all.

The weather was fair, and he went till he came to the bower: it stood open, but his wares were not to be seen: this seemed marvellous to him, so he went all round about the bower till he came

to the place whereas Helgi slept: so Roi asked
him where was his goods? but Helgi said he
knew nought of any goods he had. Roi asked
how was that. Quoth Helgi, that he had borne
out his goods at the time agreed on. "But I
saw nought of thee to fetch them away: and it
was not likely that I was going to let the things
stand there for any one to lay hands on; so I
let flit all of it away, and I call it mine and not
thine."

Roi said he dealt hastily and unjustly: "No
marvel though thou get rich speedily if thou play
such tricks as this often." Helgi said he had
gone on in that wise for some while now, and
found it availed him well enough. "But," says
he, "the king hath a case against thee whereas
thou heedest not thy goods: for it is the law of
the land, that every man shall keep his own so
that no thief may steal it, or else hath the king
a case against him: now shall the king doom
hereover." Roi said it looked little like making
money if the king must needs charge him herewith. Therewith they parted.

Then went Roi to another court, and when he
was gotten well into the garth he saw two men
coming hastily after him, and one was full like to
his late customer to look on. Roi had cast his
belt about his neck, and thereby hung that
costly knife of his. Now this first of those
twain was Thorgils, brother of Helgi: he made a
snatch at the belt as soon as they met, and said
withal: "Every man may take his own how he

may : this belt and knife thou tookest from me in Normandy, but I let smithy the things for me in England."

Said Roi : " This looks little like making money," and smiled withal. Then he went his ways and they turned back

But he had gone no long way ere he met a man, big and ill-looking, who had but one eye : so when they met Roi asked who he was ; he answered : " I ought to know thee; for I have on me a token that we have met." Roi asked what the sign might be, and the man said : " No need for thee to feign that thou knowest not : thou wert born and bred in Denmark as thou wottest, and wert a one-eyed man ; and on a time thou wentest a chaffering voyage, and layest by Samsey certain nights, whereat I chanced to be : thou hadst those men with thee, and bargained with them to bewitch me of my eye. Any man with his wits about him may see that both these eyes have been in one head : and now thou hast one, and I the other : but the king shall judge thereof to-morrow ; yea, and of thy taking the knife and belt from Thorgils my brother."

" I wot not thereof," said Roi, " but belike heavy charges are flying about to-day ; " and therewith he smiled somewhat. Therewith they parted, and Roi went to his ship : he told no man of all this, nor might any see of him but he was well content with all things.

The next morning went Roi to the town-gate,

and was all alone : and when he came thereby there was hard by a certain house wherein he heard men talking : and one took up the word, and said : "Whether will Roi the Fool come to the Thing to-morrow I wonder." Another answered : "Well, things look ugly for him, for the king ever dooms according to the urging of those brethren, whether it be right or wrong."

Roi made as if he heard not, and went his ways till he came on a young maiden going to the water, and him-seemed he had never seen a fairer woman than her : and when he came up to her she looked on him and said, "Who art thou ?"

"I am called Roi," said he.

Quoth she, "Art thou Roi the Fool ?"

He answered : "Well, belike it may now be a true name enough for me : yet have I borne, time was, a nobler name. What is thy name ?" said he.

She said : "I am called Sigrbiorg, and I am the daughter of Thorgnyr the Lawman."

Said Roi : "Fain were I to be holpen somewhat of his wisdom : but wilt thou do anything for my helping ?"

Said she : "My father hath ever little to say to men of Denmark : moreover, he is no friend to those brethren, and they have oftentimes had to bow before him."

Roi said : "But wilt thou give me some counsel herein ?"

"No man hath asked my counsel heretofore," said she, "and it is not all so sure that I know aught that may avail thee, if I were to counsel thee aught : but thou art a man to be desired, so come with me, and take thy place under my loft-bower, and take good heed to what thou hearest spoken; and that may avail thee, if any give counsel in thy case."

He said that so it should be ; and she went her ways, but Roi abode under her loft-bower.

Now Thorgnyr knew the voice of his daughter as she came into the chamber, and asked her : " What like weather is it abroad, daughter ? "

" Good is the weather," said she.

Said Thorgnyr : " Will Roi the Fool come to the Thing to-day ? "

She said she knew not.

" Why sighest thou so heavily, daughter ? " said Thorgnyr. " Hast thou met Roi the Fool ? didst thou think him a goodly man, and one to be desired ? wouldst thou give him help and furtherance ? "

She said : " Say thou now, if thou wert so grievously bestead as he is, whither thou wouldst turn to, whenas no man would take money to further thy case ? "

Thorgnyr answered : " I see nought hard to deal with herein : I would let trick meet trick : Roi will know well enow how to answer Helgi : every man may understand, that if one take another's goods by guile and treason, and do nought for him in return, the king hath a case against him, if the truth come uppermost : and he may make him a thief, and put him from all his wealth and honour ; and well may Roi pay back lie for lie—forsooth he knoweth all about this already."

She answered : " He would not be Roi the Fool were he as wise as thou : but what wouldst thou do if a man claimed the eye from out thine head?" said she, " or how wouldst thou answer him ?"

Thorgnyr answered: "Let marvel meet marvel," and therewith he told her what he would meet either case withal ; but the tale showeth hereafter what he said.

CHAPTER IV

THE STRIFE OF ROI AND HELGI

AFTER these things Sigrbiorg went away and found Roi, and asked him whether he had laid to heart that which had been counselled him; and he said he deemed he would be able to call to mind much of it.   Then she said :—

"Join thyself to my father's company when he rideth to the Thing, and heed not his hard speech though he cast but cold words at thee: for he knoweth belike that I have met thee, and that my heart yearneth toward thee; wherefore I hope that he will help thee in thy need: all the more, as he wotteth that I deem the matter to touch me closely.   But no counsel can I give thee if thou art not counselled herewith."

Therewithal they parted; and when Thorgnyr was ready he rides to the Thing, and Roi met him by the very towngate, and greeted him well.

Thorgnyr said: "Who art thou?" and Roi told of himself.

Thorgnyr said : "What would Roi the Fool in my company? go thou another road, I will not have thee with us."

Q

Roi answered: "Nay, thou wilt not spare a word to bid me follow thee, and go by the road I will, whereas there nought is to hurt thee in me, and I am a stranger here, and would fain get the good of thy company: and need enough withal driveth me on this journey, and biddeth me further my case somewhat."

So men took up the word, and said that sooth it was. So they go on till they came to the Thing, and Thorgnyr had a great company, and thither were come withal many folk of the land.

So Thorgnyr spake when men were come to the Thing: "Are those brethren, Helgi and Thorgils, come hither?"

They said yea.

"Then is it due," said Thorgnyr, "to make known to the king concerning your dealings with Roi the Fool."

Then said Helgi: "I say so much, that it was agreed between us that Roi should have all the wares that were in the bower, but I should bear them out and empty the bower; and a day was appointed for his coming back again: but I was to take in return all the lading of his ship and flit it away. And now, lord," says he, "I did according to covenant; but when I had cleared the storehouse and borne out the wares Roi was not come; so I let flit it all away, for I would not that a thief should steal it: and now I claim the goods for mine own. But I say that thou, king, hast a case against him, because he took no heed of his goods, but would have other men come to ill by his wealth : so give thou judgment, lord, concerning these things."

Said the king : "A trick was this ; yet it may be that thou wilt come by the money, if things went that road. Was such the covenant, Roi ?"

He said that he might not gainsay it. "Yet is there a flaw herein, lord : on such terms were Helgi and I agreed, when we struck the bargain, that I was to own all that was in the storehouse : and now a part of all call I creeping things, canker-worm, and moth, and all hurtful things that were therein. All these I say he should have cleared out of his storehouse, and meseems he hath not done it : and therewithal I claim Helgi as mine own ; for he was in the storehouse with me when we struck the bargain : and though he be but a sorry man, yet may I keep him for my thrall, or perchance sell him at a thrall-cheaping : so give thou judgment, lord king, concerning these things."

The king said : "With a crafty one hast thou to do now, Helgi, and no witless man."

Then said Thorgnyr : "Thou hast spoken well, Roi, and may not lightly be gainsayed : but what is to be said about thy dealings, Thorgils ?"

Thorgils answered : "I say that Roi hath taken from me knife and belt, either of them dear-bought things."

Thorgnyr said : "Then must Roi answer some-what hereto, or else confess, if he knoweth it for true."

Roi said : "Well, I will answer somewhat. I

was born and bred in Denmark, and had a brother
called Sigurd, a likelier lad than I in all wise, but
younger, as might well be seen : so on a time I
fared with him chaffering in Normandy, and he
was then twelve winters old. On a day the lad
met a man in the wood, big and straight-haired,
and they fell a-chaffering together ; and a deal of
money had got into the purse the lad bore, so
that the other had nought to give in return :
but this new-met man was keen-eyed at money,
and would have the more part of what was there,
wherefore he smote the lad to murder him, and
when men were ware thereof they came and told
me ; but when I came there my brother lay dead,
and the man was gone, and had left behind him
this knife and belt, but all the money was gone.
In such wise came I by these good things ; and I
say that Thorgils has stolen my money and slain
my brother : doom thou, lord, concerning this."

Thorgnyr said : "Surely such men as these
brethren are worthy of death."

CHAPTER V

WHAT ROI OFFERED UNTO THORIR

NOW came forward Thorir, the brother of
Helgi and Thorgils, and spake thus:
"This that appertains unto me is a hard case;"
and he told his tale, how he had lost his eye as is
afore-written. "Lord," says he, "I look to thee
to make my case good for me, for he may not
gainsay it that even so it befell as I say: and it
behoveth thee, lord, not to account outland men
of more worth than we brethren, who this long
while have been men useful to thee, and have not
slept over any matters thou hast charged us with."

The king said: "This is a marvellous matter,
and such as is seldom heard of: now, Roi, answer
thou somewhat hereto."

Answereth Roi: "I know nought of it; and
well might I show by ordeal that unsoothly it is
said of me: yet shall there be somewhat bidden
on my part for thine honour's sake, lord king."

"Let us hear it," said the king.

Said Roi: "I offer Thorir this; that the eye
be pulled out of the head of each of us, and that
the two of them be laid in the scales thereafter,

and then if they be both come out of one head, they shall be heavy alike, and I shall atone to Thorir according to thy dooming : but if Thorir will not take this, then shall he be proven a liar in more matters than this one."

Thorir said that he would not take it.

Said Thorgnyr : " Then it comes to this, that thou liest, and ye brethren do as ever wickedly and unmanly : and belike overlong ye have woven a web of lies about you, and overlong and unmeetly have been trusted of the king, who hath deemed you better men than ye were. Now is there no need to hide the truth longer about these things : for it has now become as clear as day to all that no other doom is right, but that Roi shall do his will on the life and wealth of those brethren."

Said Roi : "Soon is my doom spoken, and I shall grow no wiser about it hereafter. The brethren Thorgils and Thorir do I doom to death, their lands to thee, king, and their chattels to me : but Helgi will I have put forth from the land so that he never show his face there again, and to be taken and slain if he ever set foot in Sweden; and all his wealth I adjudge to myself."

Then were the brethren Thorgils and Thorir taken, and a gallows was raised for them, and they were hanged thereon as thieves, according to the law of the land.

So was the Thing broken up, and each man fared thence to his own home : and now was Roi called Roi the Wise.   Now he thanked Thorgnyr the Lawman for his aid, saying that he had scarce got off clear but for his counsel and wisdom. "And now," quoth he, "it may be thou wilt deem me importunate if I crave thy daughter of thee in wedlock."

Thorgnyr answered: "Well, I deem it wise to give thee a good answer herein; for betimes it was that my daughter showed me that she had set her heart upon thee to have thee."

So the wedding was done with great honour and glory, and the fairest of feasts was holden there.

Thereafter Roi arrayed him for departure, and fared to Denmark, and came to King Swein, and told him all about his voyage, and how it had gone with him : and said, that to no man was he bound to be so good as to King Swein; and therewith he gave him many good things from Sweden. King Swein said he had done well and happily, howbeit there had been close steering in the matter how it would turn out : wherewith he and the king departed, and were friends ever after while they lived. Then Roi went to Sweden, and found Thorgnyr the Lawman dead, but Thorgnyr, his son, was Lawman in his stead, and was the wisest of men: he and Roi shared the money according to the law of the land, and in all concord. Roi was accounted a right good man, and his wife had the gift of foreseeing : many noble folk in Sweden are come from them.

THE TALE OF

THORSTEIN STAFF-SMITTEN

THE TALE OF

THORSTEIN STAFF-SMITTEN

THERE was a man called Thorarin, who
dwelt in Sunnudale, an old man and feeble
of sight: he had been a red-hand viking in his
younger days, nor was he a man good to deal
with though he were old. One son he had,
hight Thorstein, a big man, sturdy, but well
ruled, who worked in such wise about his father's
house that three men else would not have turned
out more work. Thorstein was not a wealthy
man, but good weapons he had: stud-horses also
that father and son owned, that brought them in
the most of their money, whereas they would sell
away the horse-colts, who were such that they
never failed either in bottom or courage.

There was one Thord, a house-carle of Biarni
of Hof: he took heed of Biarni's riding-horses,
for a horse-learned man he was accounted. Thord
was a very unjust man, and would let many a
man feel that he was house-carle of a mighty
man: yet was he not of better worth therefor,
nor better befriended.

Two others also abode with Biarni, one named Thorhall, the other Thorvald: great tale-bearers about all that they heard in the country-side.

Now Thorstein and Thord set afoot a horse-fight for the young horses, and when they drave them together Thord's horse was put to the worse: so Thord smote Thorstein's horse on the nose with a great stroke when he saw he was getting the worst of it; which thing Thorstein saw, and smote Thord's horse in return a stroke bigger yet, so that Thord's horse ran away, and men fell a-whooping hugely.

Then Thord smote Thorstein with his horse-staff, and the stroke came on the brow so that the skin fell over the eyes. So Thorstein tore a clout from his shirt and bound up his brow, and made as if nought had happened, and bade men hide this from his father; and so the matter dropped. But Thorhall and Thorvald made a mock of this, and called him Thorstein Staff-smitten.

A little before Yule that winter the women rose up early to their work at Sunnudale, and then stood up Thorstein and bare in hay, and afterward lay down on a bench. Now cometh in old Thorarin, his father, and asked who lay there, and Thorstein told of himself.

"Why art thou so early afoot, son?" said old Thorarin.

Thorstein answered: "There are few to mate with me in the work I win here."

" Art thou not ailing in the head-bone, son ? "
said Thorarin.

" I know nought thereof," said Thorstein.

" What canst thou tell me, son, of the Horse-
meet last summer ? Wert thou not beaten into
swooning like a hound, kinsman ? "

" I think it not worth while," said Thorstein,
" to account it a stroke ; it was a chance hap
rather."

Thorarin said : " I should not have thought
it, that I could have a faint-heart for a son."

" Father," said Thorstein, " speak thou nought
but what thou wilt not think overmuch said in
time to come."

" I will not say so much as my heart would,"
said Thorarin.

Now rose up Thorstein and taketh his weapons,
and went his ways from home till he came to
the horse-house where Thord was a-heeding the
horses of Biarni, and there he found Thord.

So Thorstein came up to him and said to him :
" I would wot, friend Thord, whether that was a
chance blow that I gat from thee last summer
at the Horse-meet, or if it were done wilfully
of thee ? "

Thord answereth : " If thou hast two mouths,
thrust thou thy tongue now in one, now in the
other and call the one a chance stroke and the
other a wilful : lo, there all the boot thou gettest
of me."

" See to it," said Thorstein, " that I most like
shall not claim boot of thee again." And he fell

on him therewith and smote him his death-blow. Then he went to the house at Hof, and met a woman without and said to her: "Tell thou to Biarni that a beast hath gored Thord, his horse-boy, and that he will abide him there by the horse-house till he cometh."

"Go thy ways home, man," said she, "and I will tell it when it seemeth good to me."

So Thorstein went home and the woman went to her work.

Biarni rose up that morning, and when he was gotten to table he asked where Thord was, and men answered that he must have gone to the horses.

"I should have thought he would have been home by now if he were well," said Biarni.

Then the woman whom Thorstein had met took up the word: "True it is what is oft said of us womanfolk, that there is little of wits at work where we women are. Here came this morning Thorstein Staff-smitten, and said that a beast had gored Thord so that he might not help himself: but I was loth to wake thee, and so it slipped out of my head."

Then Biarni went from the table and out to the horse-house, and found Thord slain; and he was buried thereafter.

Biarni set a-foot a bloodsuit, and had Thorstein made guilty of the slaying: but Thorstein abode at home in Sunnudale and worked for his father, and Biarni let things be.

In the autumn sat men by the singeing-fires at Hof, but Biarni was lying outside the wall of the fire-hall, and hearkened thence the talk of men.

Now those brethren Thorhall and Thorvald take up the word: "We thought not when we first took up abode with Slaying Biarni that we should have been singeing lambs' heads here, while Thorstein, Biarni's outlaw, was singeing wethers' heads at Sunnudale: better had it been to have spared his kin something more in Bodvarsdale rather than to have let his outlaw hold his head so high in Sunnudale; but 'most men are foredone when wounds befall them :' nor wot we when he will wipe this stain from his honour."

A certain man answered: "It is worse to say such words than to hold peace over them: like it is that the trolls have set the tongues wagging in the heads of you. For we deem that Biarni is loth to take the help and sustenance from the sightless father and other helpless creatures at Sunnudale. Marvellous I shall deem it if ye are oft a-singeing lambs' heads here, or laughing over what betid in Bodvarsdale."

Now go men to table and so to sleep, and nought was it seen of Biarni that he had taken to heart what had been talked.

But the next morning Biarni waked Thorhall and Thorvald, and bade them ride to Sunnudale, and bring him at breakfast-tide the head of Thorstein sheared from his body: "For meseemeth ye are the most like to wipe the stain from my honour if I have not heart to do it myself."

Now deem they that they have assuredly spoken

overmuch, but they go their ways nevertheless till they come to Sunnudale.

Thorstein stood in the door there whetting a sax, and when they came thereto he asked them what they would, and they said they must needs seek their horses : so Thorstein said they had but a little way to seek, "For here they are by the garth."

"It is not sure," say they, "that we shall find the horses, unless thou show us of them clearly."

So Thorstein went out ; and when they were come down into the garth Thorvald hove up his axe and ran at him : Thorstein smote him with his hand so that he fell forward, and then put the sax through him. Then would Thorhall be on him, and fared in likewise with Thorvald. Then Thorstein bindeth them both a-horseback, and layeth the reins on the horses' necks, and bringeth them all on to the road, and home now go the horses to Hof.

The house-carles were without at Hof, and they go in and tell Biarni that Thorvald and his fellow were come home, and they said that they had not gone for nought. So Biarni goeth out and seeth how their dealings have gone ; and he made no words about the matter, but had them laid in earth, and all is now quiet till Yule over.

Then Rannveig took up the word one night, when they came into bed together, Biarni and she—

"What thinkest thou is most talked of in the country-side?" saith she.

"I wot not," saith Biarni: "many men are un-noteworthy of their words," saith he.

"Well," says she, "this is oftenest in men's mouths, 'What will Thorstein Staff-smitten do that thou wilt think thou must needs avenge?' He hath now slain three of thy house-carles: and thy Thingmen think that there is no upholding in thee if this be unavenged; and the hands laid on knee are ill-laid for thee."

Biarni answereth: "Now it comes to that which is said: 'None will be warned by another's woe;' yet will I hearken to what thou sayest. Few men though hath Thorstein slain sackless."

Therewith they drop this talk and sleep away the night.

On the morrow wakeneth Rannveig as Biarni took down his shield, and asked him what he would?

He answereth: "We shall shift and share honour between us in Sunnudale to-day, Thorstein and I."

"How many in company?" saith she.

"I will not drag a host against Thorstein," saith he. "I shall fare alone."

"Do it not," saith she, "to risk thyself alone under the weapons of that man of Hell!"

Said Biarni: "Yea, dost thou not after the fashion of women, bewailing now what ye egged on to then? A long while oft I bare the taunts both of thee and of others, but it will not avail to stay me when I will be afoot."

So fareth now Biarni to Sunnudale, where stood

R

Thorstein in the door, and certain words went between them. Said Biarni: "To-day shalt go with me, Thorstein, to the single-fight on yonder knoll amidst the home-mead."

"All is lacking to me," said Thorstein, "that I might fight with thee: but I will get me abroad so soon as a ship saileth; for I know of thy manliness, that thou wilt get work done for my father if I fare from him."

"It availeth not to cry off," said Biarni.

"Give me leave then to see my father first," said Thorstein.

"Yea, sure," saith Biarni.

So Thorstein went in and told his father that Biarni was come thither, who bade him to single-fight. Old Thorarin answered—

"A man must look for it if he have to do with one mightier than he, and abide in the same country-side with him, and hath done him some dishonour, that he will not live to wear out many shirts. Nor may I mourn for thee, for meseemeth thou hast earned it: so take thy weapons and do thy manliest. Time has been when I would not have budged before such as Biarni: yet is he the greatest of champions. Now would I rather lose thee than have a coward son."

So Thorstein went out, and then they went to the Knoll, and fell a-fighting eagerly, smiting the armour sorely from each other. And when they had fought a long while, Biarni said to Thorstein: "I am athirst, for I am more unwont to the work than thou."

"Go thou to the brook and drink, then," said Thorstein.

That did Biarni, and laid his sword down beside him. Thorstein took up the sword and looked on it, and said: "This sword thou wilt not have had in Bodvarsdale."

Biarni answered not, and they went up again on to the Knoll, and fought for an hour's space; and Biarni deemed the man skilled of fight, and faster on foot than he had looked for.

"Many haps hinder me to-day," said Biarni: "now is my shoe-tie loose."

"Bind it up, then," said Thorstein.

So Biarni stoops down; but Thorstein went in and brought out two shields and a sword, and went to the Knoll to Biarni, and said to him—

"Here is a shield and a sword which my father sendeth thee, and the blade will not dull more in smiting than that which thou hast had heretofore. And for me, I am loth to stand shieldless any longer before thy strokes; nay, I were fain to leave this play, for I fear me that thy luck will go further than my lucklessness: and every lad listeth to live if he may rule the rede."

"It availeth not to beg off," said Biarni; "we shall fight on yet."

"I will not smite first," said Thorstein.

Then Biarni smote away all the shield from Thorstein, and after Thorstein smote the shield from Biarni.

"A great stroke," said Biarni.

Thorstein answered: "Thine was no less."

Biarni said: "Better biteth now that same weapon of thine which thou hast borne all day afore."

Thorstein said: "I would spare myself an ill-hap if I might; and with thee I fight afeard: I will let all the matter lie under thy dooming."

And now it was Biarni's turn to smite, and they were both shieldless. So Biarni said: "It will be an ill bargain to take a crime to one instead of a good-hap: I shall deem me well paid for my three house-carles by thee alone if thou wilt be true to me."

Thorstein answereth: "Time and place served me to-day that I might have bewrayed thee, if so be my haplessness had been mightier than thy good hap: I will not bewray thee."

"I see of thee," said Biarni, "that thou art peerless among men. Give me leave to go in to thy father, and tell him such things as I will."

"Go thou in as for me," said Thorstein, "but fare thou warily."

So Biarni went in, and to the shut-bed wherein lay the carle Thorarin. Thorarin asked who went there; and Biarni named himself.

"What tidings tellest thou me, my Biarni?" said Thorarin.

"The slaying of Thorstein thy son," said Biarni.

"Made he any defence?" said Thorarin.

"I think no man hath been better man at arms than was Thorstein thy son."

"Nought wondrous," said the old man;

"though thou wert hard to deal with in Bod-varsdale if thou hast overcome my son."

Then said Biarni: "I bid thee to Hof, and thou shalt sit in the second high-seat whiles thou livest, and I will be to thee in a son's stead."

"So it fareth with me," said the old man, "as with them who have no might, that: 'Oft is the fool fain of promise.' But such are the promises of you great men, when ye will appease a man after such haps as this, that it is a month's rest to us, and thereafter are we held even as worthy as other poor wretches, and no sooner for all that do our sorrows wear out. Nevertheless, he who taketh handsel of such a man as thee may be well content with his lot, when matters are to be doomed on; and this handsel will I take of thee. So come thou on to my shut-bed floor, and draw very nigh, for the old carle tottereth on his feet now with eld and feebleness; nor deem it so but my dead son yet runneth in my head."

So Biarni went up on to the shut-bed floor, and took old Thorarin by the hand, and found him fumbling with a sax which he had a mind to thrust into Biarni. So he drew aback his hand and said: "Wretchedest of old carles! now shall it go as meet is betwixt us! Thorstein thy son lives, and shall home with me to Hof: but I will get thee thralls to work for thee, nor shalt thou want for aught whiles thou livest."

So Thorstein fared home to Hof with Biarni, and served him till his death-day, and was deemed peerless of any man for manhood and courage.

Biarni kept his honour still, and waxed ever in friendship and good conditions the older he grew; and was the best proven of all men, and was a man of great faith in his latter days. He fared abroad and went south, and in that journey died, and resteth in the burg called Valeri, a little way hitherward from Rome-town. Biarni was a man happy of kin : his son was Skeggbroddi, much told of in tale, a man peerless in his days.

So here an end of telling of Thorstein Staff-smitten.

NOTES

NOTES

THE TALE OF HOGNI AND HEDINN
(pp. 201–225)

From the Skáldskaparmál, Chap. 50

BATTLE is called the Tempest or Storm of the Host of Hedinn, and weapons are called the Fires of the Host of Hedinn, or the Wands of the Host of Hedinn : but this is the story told thereof :—

A king, who is named Hogni, had a daughter hight Hild, whom a king hight Hedinn, son of Hiarandi, took as a prey of war whenas King Hogni was gone to an assembly of the kings; who, when he heard that there was war in his realm, and that his daughter was borne away, fared with his host a-seeking Hedinn, and heard of him that he had sailed north along the land. But when King Hogni came to Norway, he heard that Hedinn had sailed west over the sea; so Hogni sailed after him, right away to the Orkneys, and when he came to the island called Há, there was Hedinn before him with his company.

Then fared Hild to her father, and offered him a necklace as atonement on Hedinn's part; and said that on the other hand Hedinn was all ready to fight, and that Hogni need look for no sparing from him. Hogni answered his daughter roughly, and when she met Hedinn she told him that Hogni would have no peace, and bade him array him for battle. And so they did, either of them, and went up on to the island, and ordered their hosts. Then called Hedinn to Hogni his father-in-law, and bade him peace, and much gold in atonement.

Then answered Hogni : " Over-late hast thou bidden this, if thou wilt have peace ; for now have I drawn Dāinsloom whom the Dwarfs wrought, who shall be a man's bane every time he is bare, and never faltereth in his stroke, and no hurt that cometh of him healeth."

Then answereth Hedinn : "The sword thou art praising, and not the victory. A good sword I call it that clings to its master."

Then began they that battle which is called the Slaughter of the Host of Hedinn, and fought all that day, and at night-tide the Kings fared to their ships.

But in the night went Hild to the field of the slain, and woke up by witchcraft all them that were dead ; and the next day went the Kings to the field of battle and fought, and all they withal who had fallen the day before.

So fared that battle day after day, that they that fell, and all weapons and armour of defence that lay on the field of battle, turned to stone ; but when day dawned stood up all the dead men and fought, and all the weapons were of avail again. And so is it said in songs, that in this wise shall the Host of Hedinn abide the Doom of the Gods.

NOTE TO PAGE 54, *l.* 28

T HE sittings of the three Things referred to took place under the following dates :—

The most thronged, following the burning of Njal and his sons, took place A.D. 1012.

The next in time and point of multitude was that at which the so-called Heath-slaughters were atoned for, A.D. 1015.

The last in point of multitude, but first in time, was that mentioned in our Saga, which took place in 1006.

INDEX

INDEX

TO THE STORY OF GUNNLAUG THE WORM-TONGUE

₊ *The number signifies the page*

INDEX

TO THE STORIES OF FRITHIOF THE BOLD, VIGLUND THE FAIR, HOGNI AND HEDINN, ROI THE FOOL, AND THORSTEIN STAFF-SMITTEN

THE END

WORKS BY WILLIAM MORRIS.

POETICAL WORKS.

LIBRARY EDITION.

Complete in Eleven Volumes.   Crown 8vo, price 5s. net each.

THE EARTHLY PARADISE.   4 vols.   5s. net each.

THE LIFE AND DEATH OF JASON.   5s. net.

THE DEFENCE OF GUENEVERE, AND OTHER POEMS.   5s. net.

THE STORY OF SIGURD THE VOLSUNG, AND THE FALL OF THE NIBLUNGS.   5s. net.

LOVE IS ENOUGH; OR, THE FREEING OF PHARAMOND: A Morality; and POEMS BY THE WAY.   5s. net.

THE ODYSSEY OF HOMER.   Done into English Verse.   5s. net.

THE AENEIDS OF VIRGIL.   Done into English Verse.   5s. net.

THE TALE OF BEOWULF, SOMETIME KING OF THE FOLK OF THE WEDERGEATS.   Translated by WILLIAM MORRIS and A. J. WYATT.   Crown 8vo, 5s. net.

Certain of the POETICAL WORKS may also be had in the following Editions:—

THE EARTHLY PARADISE.   Popular Edition.   5 vols.   12mo, 25s.; or 5s. each, sold separately.

The same in Ten Parts, 25s.; or 2s. 6d. each, sold separately.

Cheap Edition, in One Volume.   Crown 8vo, 6s. net.

POEMS BY THE WAY.   Square crown 8vo, 6s.

THE LIFE OF WILLIAM MORRIS.

BY J. W. MACKAIL.

With 6 Portraits, and 16 Illustrations by E. H. NEW, etc.
2 vols.   8vo, 32s.

LONGMANS, GREEN, AND CO.
LONDON, NEW YORK, AND BOMBAY.

WORKS BY WILLIAM MORRIS.

PROSE WORKS.

THE SUNDERING FLOOD. Crown 8vo, 7s. 6d.

THE WOOD BEYOND THE WORLD. Crown 8vo, 6s. net.

THE WATER OF THE WONDROUS ISLES. Crown 8vo, 7s. 6d.

THE WELL AT THE WORLD'S END. 2 vols. 8vo, 28s.

THE STORY OF THE GLITTERING PLAIN, which has been also called The Land of the Living Men, or The Acre of the Undying. Square post 8vo, 5s. net.

THE ROOTS OF THE MOUNTAINS, wherein is told somewhat of the Lives of the Men of Burgdale, their Friends, their Neighbours, their Foemen, and their Fellows-in-Arms. Written in Prose and Verse. Square crown 8vo, 8s.

A TALE OF THE HOUSE OF THE WOLFINGS, and all the Kindreds of the Mark. Written in Prose and Verse. Square crown 8vo, 6s.

THE STORY OF GRETTIR THE STRONG. Translated from the Icelandic by EIRÍKR MAGNÚSSON and WILLIAM MORRIS. Crown 8vo, 5s. net.

THREE NORTHERN LOVE STORIES, AND OTHER TALES. Translated from the Icelandic by EIRÍKR MAGNÚSSON and WILLIAM MORRIS. Crown 8vo, 6s. net.

A DREAM OF JOHN BALL, AND A KING'S LESSON. 12mo, 1s. 6d.

NEWS FROM NOWHERE; OR, AN EPOCH OF REST. Being some Chapters from an Utopian Romance. Post 8vo, 1s. 6d.

SIGNS OF CHANGE. Seven Lectures delivered on various Occasions. Post 8vo, 4s. 6d.

HOPES AND FEARS FOR ART. Five Lectures delivered in Birmingham, London, etc., in 1878–1881. Crown 8vo, 4s. 6d.

AN ADDRESS DELIVERED AT THE DISTRIBUTION OF PRIZES TO STUDENTS OF THE BIRMINGHAM MUNICIPAL SCHOOL OF ART ON 21ST FEBRUARY 1894. 8vo, 2s. 6d. net.

ART AND THE BEAUTY OF THE EARTH: a Lecture delivered at Burslem Town Hall, on October 13, 1881. 8vo, 2s. 6d. net.

SOME HINTS ON PATTERN-DESIGNING: a Lecture delivered at the Working Men's College, London, on 10th December 1881. 8vo, 2s. 6d. net.

ARCHITECTURE AND HISTORY; and WESTMINSTER ABBEY. Two Papers written for the Society for the Protection of Ancient Buildings, 1884 and 1893. 8vo, 2s. 6d. net.

ARTS AND CRAFTS ESSAYS. By Members of the Arts and Crafts Exhibition Society. With a Preface by WILLIAM MORRIS. Crown 8vo, 2s. 6d. net.

LONGMANS, GREEN, AND CO.
LONDON, NEW YORK, AND BOMBAY.

Lightning Source UK Ltd.
Milton Keynes UK
UKOW02f0832070616

275785UK00001B/24/P